GHOSTS AND GOBLINS AND AND MURDER

Book Four: The Fiona Fleming Cozy Mysteries

PATTI LARSEN

CHAPTER ONE

THREE KIDS UNDER THE age of ten crowded the front of the table with their hopeful expressions and plates held high. I dutifully doled out chunks of Mom's elaborate creation, the cake now a ravaged wasteland of Halloween décor goodness, and grinned as the cuteness patrol in costume all said, "thank you!" at exactly the same moment before bobbing off with their second helping.

So adorable. And I was delighted I didn't have to take them—or their pending sugar high—home with me, thank you very much.

Petunia grumbled at my feet, shifting her weight from one front paw to the other, licking her lips in that smacking way of hers, lines of drool dripping from her muzzle. One thin strand landed on the toe of my pointed witch shoe, gleaming in the industrial lighting of the community center's fluorescents, dark brown eyes bulging more than usual. The rims of white showed so much I worried she might pop a socket.

"You, missy," I said, shaking the serving spatula at her, "have had enough cake to last you the rest of your pug lifetime."

She moaned, her fat fawn body wriggling inside her ghost costume. I should have left her home at my B&B of the same name, but I didn't have the heart. Especially when Mom went and bought her the adorable outfit I'd dutifully stuffed Petunia into.

One of the kids squealed, the smack of cake hitting the floor sending the pug skittering off, trailing her white hem behind her, already stained along the bottom by previous encounters with the black and red icing Mom slathered on her creepy diorama design. I sighed, not even bothering to call after my dog this time, knowing it wouldn't do me any good. Mind you, neither would the diabetic coma she'd fall into if I let this go on much longer.

And the farting? Would be legendary.

Daisy looked up from a small group of kids who she directed in a game of apple bobbing and grinned like she was having the time of her life. My best friend's new venture into event planning had quickly overtaken her short stint in real estate. I never did get the full story behind her rapid flight from the offices of Pat and Ashley Champville three short weeks into her job. But I'd heard enough rumors about accidental pricing discounts on legal documents that amounted to a very inexpensive purchase I knew better than to ask for further details.

It seemed, though, after bouncing from one career opportunity to the next that Daisy had finally found something she truly loved. She looked stunning in her princess dress and tiara, fairytale heroine leading the kids around like she'd cast a spell on them while their happy parents looked on. This Halloween party had been meant to happen at my place, her first self-created event. But it had grown in size and attendance so quickly she'd had no trouble convincing our mayor to let her use the community center at town hall instead.

Just as well. I couldn't imagine the cleanup at my B&B if I had to host all these kids and their sticky fingers.

More squealing, this time off to the right where Daisy had set up the Tunnel of Terror. The curtained off pathway hosted volunteers inside who wickedly scared the living crap out of the kids as they maneuvered their way through. There was a lineup, naturally. I shook my head, smiling as I turned to dish up more cake to a small turtle and his fireman companion, knowing that my dad was likely having as much fun as the kids he scared.

Who knew the tough-as-nails man's man John Fleming, former sheriff and all around tower of stoic sternness, could giggle like a little kid?

I sighed over the remnants of Mom's beautiful cake, the red velvet interior smelling divine, the last few headstones and a single fondant tree remaining of the graveyard scene, though the crispy castle and the moat of pudding remained. I considered stealing a piece to take home as Petunia waddled her way back to me, sitting at my feet once more, burping abruptly before panting at me like she wouldn't be throwing up later.

I felt a bit badly for our mayor, Olivia Walker, and her photo op booth, but honestly, she came dressed in her typical suit, her only nod to the holiday an orange shirt under her dark brown dress jacket.

Oh, and a pair of tiny bat earrings I'm sure she had custom made. She'd been under so much pressure I worried about her, saw the strain in her face as she sat very still and stiff, sleek black hair a match to her rigid expression, smiling like it was plastered on. It must have irked her to be ignored, the kids screaming and running and generally having a great time that didn't require anything as formal as a sit down with our mayor. Like she thought she was Halloween Santa or something.

Still, she'd done so much for our town since she took over it was hard to judge her. Okay, not so hard, I'd done some myself, fair enough. Her drive to attract tourism to Reading had succeeded, but not without cost. Things were booming, to the point our town overflowed with visitors, though I wondered sometimes if we might lose sight of who we were if the kind of growth and expansion happening continued at the rate it was. My friend, Jared Wilkins, was at wits end these days, though it was a happy set of troubles to have too many projects to build and not enough workers or time to get them done. At least his father's terrible business practices didn't hurt in the end. Jared made everything right that he could, and considering his dad was an utter fraud and a jerk, having a local boy step up meant a lot.

I dolloped some cake onto a little pirate's plate, grinning. "Argh, Captain. How's the party?"

She looked at me like I'd cracked my walnut and scooted off. At least I tried. Just like Olivia had, bringing up all the pirate treasure stuff despite the fact the hoard of Captain Reading had long been debunked. The idea that the founder of our town hid his gold and jewels somewhere in the area had long been rumored, and equally contested. Olivia's statue to Reading and her summer spent doing her best to use the old wives' tale to her advantage had pretty much bombed.

I shrugged off the fact my now deceased Grandmother Iris left me clues to that very treasure. There was a good chance it was a goose chase and I'd pretty much shelved it for the time being. Without any kind of lead past the scrap of map and the doubloon sitting in the music box she left me, I had, at best, bits and pieces of what amounted to a fun story to tell.

Except, of course, I hadn't told anyone yet, outside of Daisy. Silly, but I loved having the secret to myself.

The curtain in the far corner moved aside, the

beads rattling as one of the parents departed, looking shaken but grinning. I rolled my eyes at myself, at the fortune teller booth and the second woman who emerged, dressed like some kind of gypsy who'd clearly been born colorblind and without anything resembling taste. Yes, it was Halloween. Except that the few times I'd seen her around town, Sadie Hatch had been dressed pretty much just like she was right now.

I quickly looked away, hoping she wouldn't notice me, though I knew it was rude. There was just something about her that gave me the creeps. When she'd moved to Reading a year ago, Daisy begged me to go with her to a séance or something equally ridiculous and I'd turned her down. But from what I'd heard the older woman who claimed to be some kind of psychic was doing a cracking business, so good for her.

I stared down at the cake again, mouth watering. Surely I could just sneak a piece. Mom would make me one of my very own, I knew that without asking. She'd be delighted, in fact. There was nothing Lucy Fleming loved more than being in the kitchen, creating with confections. But it wasn't the promise of a cake later that appealed.

It was cake *now*.

"Time is passing," a voice said, deep and raspy. I turned with a little gasp to come face-to-face with none other than our local soothsayer. Sadie's thin lips were turned down, her eyebrows drawn into thin arches over her sagging lids, pale eyes washed out but sharp and observant. She waved one hand at me, the tinkle of her bangles giving me goosebumps. Or maybe it was the clashing red sash she wore with that hideous green and purple striped skirt, topped by a dark orange blouse and a shawl of rainbow hues?

I'd be going with that for the trigger.

"Cake?" Yes, I seriously just offered her a slice, the spatula hovering, a weak smile on my lips as I silently begged her to just leave already.

She ignored my suggestion, leaning closer, the smell of incense strong in her gray hair. Sadie came maybe to my shoulder, but there was bulk to her under her clothes, and for some odd reason intimidation rose off her in waves.

"Your window closes," she said then. "For progeny of your own." She leaned away, sniffed, nodded. "Act within two years or you are doomed to a life alone."

I gaped, spatula dripping red crumbs onto

Petunia's head, absorbing what the old woman said, a ball of cold shock bursting in my stomach.

She did *not* just tell me my biological clock was ticking.

I swear she was this close to being smacked in the face with cake. But before I could overcome my stunned lack of ability to act, a young man approached in a hurry, meeting my eyes in a brief, embarrassed flicker before he grasped her arm and tugged.

"Grandma," he said. "The Cortez's are here."

Sadie swept past him, shaking off his hand, hurrying without seeming to toward the tall, handsome couple waiting at the door. Her departure was as abrupt as her arrival, like she'd delivered that hideously inappropriate message for my sake or because the stupid spirits told her to or some other absolutely horrendous excuse to make a total stranger feel like crap about herself and was now done with me, leaving me to crumble like a piece of the very cake I served into a mound of regretful and wailing horror of where I'd failed.

The most frustrating part of the entire encounter, despite knowing better and being a self-made woman with her own choices and life to live and screw what anyone else thought including a hideous old fortune teller who could kiss my ass?

It worked. As I watched her interact with the grim-faced, bearded man and the softly weeping woman, their height and slim fitness and glowing golden skin a contrast to her hunched pale creepiness, I felt myself wither inside.

There was only one thing that could make things worse. And, naturally, because that's my luck, right? That one thing happened a heartbeat after Sadie exited with the couple following, her grandson slouching quietly after her. As I fought tears and frustration and the need to throw the spatula in my hand to the ground, a stunning blonde in a dress, hat and shoes that cost more than my jewelry collection stepped into my line of sight. Looked my thrown-together variation of her costume up and down. And smiled.

Vivian French just had to come to the party as a witch, too.

CHAPTER TWO

I KNEW WHAT SHE was thinking, the nasty piece of work who pretended she owned Reading because her parents left her their stupid bakery. It was written all over her smug ass face, and made my stomach clench in anxious response. Not because I considered her more successful than I was. Petunia's was incredibly busy. Sure, I might not have had three locations thriving in other states—big whoop, who needed the work? No, it had nothing to do with the competitive itch I refused to scratch when it came to Vivian and me.

Instead, it was a much older hurt that woke in that moment, one I had no idea I still clung to but likely would have admitted if I was willing to examine why I really didn't like her.

We were dressed as witches. Both of us. Again. The re-creation of our seventh grade conflict—and honestly, as far as I can recall, the first time she bullied me personally—we'd come to Jana Hamlin's Halloween party dressed like witches. Sure, Vivian had a hate on for me since I'd broken her nose the year before, defending Daisy who didn't even realize the mean girl blonde was being cruel to her. I'd seen it, though, acted without thinking and made a best friend that day.

I guess I should have expected retaliation. It never came, lulled me into a false sense of victory. At least, until that night. The flashback was so vivid I felt myself shudder.

I'd begged until Mom bought me the coveted outfit I'd seen hanging in a store window in Burlington. Couldn't wait to show it off. Walked through the door at Jana's, strolled into the living room. And froze in stunned silence at the sight of blonder, prettier, skinnier, more popular Vivian French. Dressed in my exact costume.

I flinched at the memory that flashed through my mind. And though it seemed to take ages for it to unwind, I know it was literally a second, the briefest of moments. Enough, though, to churn my knotted stomach into a cesspool of dread though the resulting verbal and emotional assault she'd clearly perfected elsewhere as fresh to my twenty-nine-year-old heart as if it was happening right now, all over again.

Didn't help I was already vulnerable, thanks to Sadie Damned Hatch, did it?

Vivian tossed her ringletted blonde hair, the sparkles over her eyebrows catching the horribly harsh light as she arched one at me, augmented lashes and blue eyes making her look like an artificial creation, not human at all. Cold, crisp, judging. And in a moment of weakness where neither of us said a word, I failed myself. Let her judge me, absorbed her disdain, made it my own.

Because I'm an idiot like that sometimes.

When she finally spoke, her slow up and down intake of my outfit making me feel shabby and worthless—thanks, ego, I really needed that smack in the head—her cool, disinterested tone shoved me further down the hole I'd found myself in.

What the hell was wrong with me?

"What an... interesting cake choice." Of course she'd go after Mom's creation. She'd been nothing but a critical crab ass since she found out Mom had started creating confections for those who would have normally bought from Vivian's bakery. The self-anointed Queen of Wheat (okay, I anointed her that because it was funny at the time) and owner of French's Handmade Bakery, hated that my talented mother might cut into her business.

That at least got my temper up, cut through the haze of self-judgment I'd been wallowing in since the old soothsayer had the nerve to slice my confidence and happiness in half.

"The kids love it." I was pretty proud of my own deadpan, level tone. Good for me.

Vivian's delicate shrug ruffled her floof of a skirt, making her tight corset crinkle faintly, a few sparkles falling from her narrow, tanned shoulders.

"Common tastes," she said. "Typical of Reading."

Wow. She'd find out just how common when I punched her in the face and broke her nose again. I don't condone violence, honestly. Didn't stop me from clinging to the recollection of smacking her a good one—ah, memories, how fun—while she went on.

"I see your own tastes weren't improved during your New York hiatus." She did the up and down again, a faint smile artfully created, cultivated. Hit the mark, too, and I just barely cut off my involuntary reaction to smooth my layered scarf skirt, my teased hair. Not giving her the satisfaction even if I choked on it.

I didn't comment. I knew if I opened my mouth to speak, my voice would shake and I was not giving her that. My entire existence narrowed down to the two of us, a tunnel of darkness in my vision leading only to the stunning vision of Vivian French, my heart beating so fast I felt sweat begin to moisten my upper lip.

No. I might have been unravelling as we stared at each other and I might spend the evening crying over cake after the fact, but she would not see me crack here and now. Not ever.

"Well," she said at last, a million years later. Was that disappointment in her eyes? Then I'd succeeded. Yay, Fleming. "Now that I've seen what Reading's new event coordinator has to offer, I'll be going." More disdain, this time for Daisy.

It was the first moment I took firm hold of myself and asked what Vivian was up to. Why was she here, standing in front of me, doing her best to belittle and unnerve me when we'd mostly avoided each other like the plague since I moved home?

It was enough to crack the surface of the poor me bubble of darkness I'd been falling into, and jerked me back into reality.

"Besides," she said, smile widening into something distinctly savage, "I'm meeting the lovely Sheriff Turner for coffee and I'd hate to be late."

Not *my* Crew. Yes, I thought of him as mine even though he hadn't asked me out yet and I'd been so patient with the handsome widower who seemed to like me, but damn him. Damn him. Coffee with Vivian, of all people? Like, a date? When he'd promised me he'd ask when he was ready, when he was done grieving his beloved wife?

Choke.

Vivian was a liar. The initial stab to the heart passed as quickly as my refusal to accept anything she said as truth shook me abruptly. It was there in her eyes, in the calculated way she watched me as she pushed each and every button she could dig up. She'd be mentioning my cheating ex, Ryan Richards, shortly, my failure and New York already part of the conversation. Or some other taunt to twist me into knots.

I was so done with this conversation. Before I

could think, I acted, turning abruptly to hack a massive slice from the black fondant graveyard, whipping around with crumbs flying, beaming a smile. "Cake?"

She had no idea how close she was to wearing it.

I don't know where she came from or how long she'd observed our little conversation from hell, but the only thing that saved Vivian from a face full of red velvet was Daisy. She appeared out of nowhere, slipping in between me and the hideous creature hiding behind blue eyes and sparkles, her height and curvaceous figure easily outgunning the bakery queen. Vivian's face snapped to irritation but she backed off as my best friend beamed at her, hands clasping in front of her while she looked Vivian up and down much as the witch had done to me.

"Why, Vivs," she gushed, "what a treat! Thank you for coming. But this is a costume party." She tsked with fake chastisement, as if the blonde were one of the little girls running around, unhinged and over sugared. "But nice effort!"

Vivian didn't respond, flat, furious expression crackling over her perfect face. She spun and marched away, the too-short flounce of her gigantic skirt bobbing, skinny legs sticking out beneath.

"Looks like a chicken from the back," Daisy said with faint concern. "Poor thing needs to eat a sandwich."

I gasped a half-laugh, half-sob, setting down my spatula and turning away so she wouldn't see how close I was to crying. Don't get me wrong, I appreciated the rescue, but the fact I'd almost lost it in front of Vivian of all people... I was better than this.

Daisy tried to talk, but I shook my head, instead plastering on a fake smile and continuing to hand out dessert, though I think my lingering attitude scared a few kids away. Oh well, more cake for me.

Forty-five minutes later, as the party wrapped up, I hastily cleaned my station with more aggression than necessary, no further along the path to recovering from my encounters than I was when they happened. I pretended I didn't see Daisy and Mom, Dad assisting, tearing down the tunnel curtains. I just wasn't in the right headspace to join their laughter.

Great party. Could I go home now, please?

"Fiona, dear." Olivia's visit was the last thing I needed. I turned partway around, hands full of dirty plates and the partially eaten bits of sculpted haunted house I prepped to toss in the trash, knowing I probably didn't look welcoming but pretty much over being here already. "Come to my office at some point. I have something to discuss with you that may be to our mutual advantage." She didn't specify or even seem to notice I had other things on my mind than her agenda, but marched away, head high. As if she'd had a lovely time and wasn't this just the best party ever?

Grunt. Whatever she wanted, I was about as far from caring as I could get and might never be in the mood to "discuss" at this rate. Olivia's scheming might have been helpful, but she'd been declining in popularity and I had no doubt she was on the edge of desperation to get herself back into the good graces of the council. While I understood such motivation, I had no desire to get wrapped up in whatever it was she had in mind next. I'd already earned a reputation as a nosy busybody who had terrible luck when it came to dead people. The last thing I wanted at this point was to exacerbate talk about my character by siding with Olivia when she was on the way out.

Wow, that was callous and really not like me. I blamed it on the bad day I'd been having and went back to work.

Choosing to conveniently forget Olivia's sort of

offer, kind of command, I finished cleaning with a sigh, wrapping up a piece of cake for myself with sad determination to eat the whole thing as fast as I could the second I got home before getting into pajamas and climbing under the covers to watch TV until I stopped the urge to cry myself into throwing up.

Great plan. Sold.

CHAPTER THREE

IT WAS HARDER THAN I thought to avoid Mom, Dad and Daisy on my way out, but I managed. I did feel a bit wretched about not staying to finish the full clean up, but I just couldn't be in public anymore. Petunia panted next to me as I walked the few blocks home, head down, giant hat in one hand, cake clutched in the other, the loop of my pug's leash around my wrist. Not like I needed to leash her. She could barely run, so even if she did take off she'd make it all of five steps before her fat butt collapsed from the effort. Still, it was comforting to be linked to her like this.

And I needed all the comfort I could get right about now. Pathetic, but true.

Was my biological clock ticking? I blinked as burning in the corners of my eyes told me I very well might have been suppressing such thoughts. It wasn't like I longed for kids or anything. It was true I'd been feeling a bit on the lonely side lately, but I'd also been crazy busy, too. Running a bed and breakfast wasn't exactly the kind of lifestyle conducive to meeting a life partner. There were a lot of weeks, months even, I barely had time to shower let alone make space for love. Hard not to accept that I'd been dragging my feet, though, since my ex's devastating actions sent me scurrying back home to Reading. I wondered if Ryan was still with whatever-her-name-was or if he'd cheated on her and moved on already.

Whatever. She could have him. They deserved each other. And, if there was a goddess out there looking out for women like me, Ryan's side-chick cheated on him this time and he was the one who ended up with the broken heart. Not much of a hope there, but I still used it some nights to keep me warm.

If I was going to be totally honest with myself— and when wasn't I?—I had to admit being the strong, independent businesswoman, while a great example for young women, didn't do much for me in the heart department. I didn't need a partner, but… but. It would have been nice.

Who was I kidding? I was so over being alone. Not enough to go for just anyone, or to make another mistake like I had with Ryan. Alone still sucked, though.

There were lots of women out there who balanced a great job and/or business of their own, kids and a spouse, though, weren't there? So I could try to blame me being busy for my present state all I wanted, blame Ryan for cheating for making me reticent to try again. I could keep lying to myself, or I could stop waiting for Crew Turner to ask me out and find someone who wasn't emotionally unavailable. Unless, of course, waiting meant I was just as screwed up as he was.

There was some happy thinking.

I'd made it barely a block, the self-flagellation of my slow plod home in full swing, when the whole horrible experience of the last hour came to a stunning and inevitable head. Maybe I was asking for it, thinking about myself the way I did, or maybe it was just coincidence. But whatever the role fate played in that moment, I was just stepping into the crosswalk when a sheriff's car pulled up, the driver's window rolling down and my cousin Robert—thick black mustache and smarmy grin and all—came to a halt beside me.

"Fanny." He winked, easing the car forward as I kept walking, refusing to look him in the eye. "How's the local busybody? Have anyone die on you lately?" My most despised extended family member had become a deputy out of high school because I couldn't. And made sure I knew it at graduation, too. While I normally brushed off his pathetic attempts to hurt me, I'd fallen again into the Fee Sucks fan club. Meaning his use of my hated nickname from high school cut like a knife. Not to mention the jab about my unfortunate penchant for my proximity to the recently deceased.

"Aren't you supposed to be working?" Wow, that was a great insult, Fee. Way to muster anything resembling wit and cold disdain. Best I could do considering I'd used up my best material on myself already.

Robert must have sensed I was down and out, because he seized on the opportunity to strike. "Just saying," he grinned. "No one likes a snoop, Fanny." He chuckled to himself while I internalized his insults and added them to the litany against me despite my best efforts not to.

Apparently my lack of response wasn't what he had in mind. "Looks like you didn't take my advice last spring. That ass is bigger than ever." With that insult added to hurt, he decided to add injury to the list of offerings. Before I knew what was happening, he reached out his driver's window and smacked me.

Smacked. My. Butt.

I stopped abruptly, staring at him in shock but unable to do anything. Not react, not lash out. Nada, the big el zilcho, thanks for playing.

He seemed to take my silence as some kind of attack, though, and flinched suddenly, paling. Like he knew he'd gone too far at last. "Be seeing you, Fanny," he said before he peeled out, cutting off a car coming behind him, laying on his horn when they beeped their protest.

I stood there in the crosswalk, stunned and unable to move, until a pickup truck tooted impatiently for me to get moving. Which I did, in a lurching kind of startled reaction, certain I'd still be standing there, growing roots in the street, if the driver hadn't come along.

Maybe Robert knew he'd crossed a line—I could easily have reported him for assault. That could get him fired. I knew Dad would back me and that Crew would. Or would he? I plodded on, startled but unable to stop when I realized I was crying silently, tears landing on the plastic wrapped cake I clutched to my chest.

Petunia's soft whine broke sorrow's hold as she looked up at me, clearly aware something was wrong. I stopped again, this time out of traffic, and scratched one of her ears, hearing her moan softly in delight at the attention, the last of my tears making bright, shining beads on her fawn coat.

"I have nothing to feel badly about." I wiped at my face before heading for home again, forcing my shoulders back. "I have a great life." I did, too. "I'm just fine on my own, aren't I?" I looked down at Petunia who panted happily back. "Besides, I have you." Yup, my pug counted.

A bench beckoned and rather than drag my pathetic and apparently fat butt back home just yet, I sat on the street side with my pug at my feet and proceeded to eat my cake with my fingers, feeding bits to the already full—and yet eternally empty—dog beside me.

"It's silly to feel this way, Petunia," I said, quietly, though there was no one else around to overhear me.

"What is wrong with people?" I picked at the remains of the cake, not even wanting it, really, setting it aside with a sigh, mind still going in circles. "*Is* Sadie right?" Though I'd never been one to go looking for confrontation, it was apparent I needed to confront this or let it ruin the rest of my day. And maybe my life. "Is my clock ticking?" I looked down at Petunia who licked her chops, head tilting, black ears perked. She muttered something in pugspeak and I nodded. "I'm twenty-nine," I said, remembering my brief party last month when Daisy, Mom and Dad and the Jones ladies sang me a quick rendition of the birthday song in between guest arrivals, no time for a proper celebration. "So I guess it might be." Did I even want kids? Maybe. Someday. With the right person. Or even alone if I decided that was the way I wanted to go. But I didn't realize until she'd brought it up just how alone I'd been feeling. "So it's true. I've been waiting for Crew." I accepted that finally. He hadn't asked me to. In fact, he said when he was ready to date again, if I was free, we'd give it a try.

My ridiculous little heart took that statement and made it all about waiting for him to hurry up and ask me. Instead of moving on. Though, to be honest, there wasn't much in the form of potential here in town. Didn't mean I couldn't consider someone in a nearby community, though.

No longer drowning in my own angst, I rose, depositing the remains of my cake in the trash can beside the bench—to Petunia's horror—and finally went home, feeling a bit better and with a plan, at least. To stop waiting and accept that there was a good chance "my" Crew might never be ready. Or, that when he was, I was firmly determined not to be.

Vivian could have him. I just wished I believed I wouldn't die of jealousy if that was how this story ended.

CHAPTER FOUR

THE HOUSE FELT EMPTY to me as I entered, the big grandfather clock in the foyer chiming 4PM as I walked through the door. I was without guests the next two days, a rarity since I'd taken over the B&B, and a welcome bit of quiet, to be honest. The next two months were fully booked, right to the first week of January, this odd little lull the perfect window for me to catch my breath, get some minor things finished to the house and recoup my energy before the next wave of excited tourists rolled through Reading.

No complaints, honest.

But typically the house would at least have two bodies in it before 5PM. I paused in the entry,

Petunia free from her leash to wander down the hall toward the kitchen, and had to remind myself there was a perfect timing fairy and that she had my best interests at heart. Because this was the week Mary and Betty Jones were both out, my two elderly employees taking time off so the more silent of the two could have knee surgery. Naturally, Mary had to be with her the entire time, since the two were never apart. Though Betty wasn't exactly a great conversationalist and Mary had grunting, ancient opinions about things that made me eye roll at times, I missed their presence.

Yes, yes. It wasn't lost on me, this feeling of being alone all over again. Sigh.

I followed my pug to the door to the kitchen and swung it open, letting her precede me. She continued on toward the back door, the doggy flap just barely big enough to accommodate her girth. Every effort I'd made to cut down her weight ended in failure thanks to the sisters, my parents and Daisy. Pretty much everyone who loved her fed her things she wasn't supposed to have.

Including me, at least today. She'd be pooping red velvet for weeks.

Knowing I'd have to go outside eventually and

clean up her deposit—at least she hadn't started farting yet, there was a silver lining that would turn black and revolting by the time we went to bed—I instead tossed my witch hat to the back of one of the stools at the counter and leaned against the tall, tiled surface. Mom had been here earlier to finish her prep for the party, but you'd never know it. To my relief, she and Dad volunteered to help me out while the sisters were gone and I'd be needing them in short order. Nice to have them around so much.

I spent the rest of the afternoon and evening poking around the B&B, trying to muster the energy to tackle any number of small jobs. I needed to repaint the front steps at some point, and room six could use a new number, the old one rather tarnished. There were always emails to check, the website to update. I simply couldn't focus, drifting from one thing to the next until darkness fell, the tired pug who followed me around yawning and tooting, grumbling about still being up and around though it was only early yet.

We ended up where I'd feared we would, in bed, the TV on though I didn't really watch much, flipping through channels while Petunia snored happily at my side. When I finally hit the power button and sighed, staring at the ceiling, I had to admit I was depressed.

Not hard core, give me meds, hysterical calls to my therapist depressed. Just… blue.

This wasn't me. And yet, as I lay there, more tears trickling down my temples into my hair, a faint hitch in my breath, I realized it was.

I turned over abruptly, a change of scenery necessary. My gaze caught and settled on the music box sitting on my side table. I reached for it, touched the top with the tips of my fingers, stroking the soft, red velvet inlay before I lifted the lid and listened to the familiar song tinkling from within, the tiny ballerina turning endlessly in response.

It was inevitable I'd open the secret compartment, examine the map piece with its off-center compass, the gold doubloon heavy in my hand, image stamped into it faded to a faint impression. Though exciting at the time, I hated that this mystery hit a dead end like it did. Maybe the Reading horde was a real thing and maybe it wasn't. Leaving this unresolved just added to my sense of gloom.

I fell asleep in a terrible state of mind. And woke the next morning crabby and out of sorts. Awesome.

Instead of allowing myself to wallow further, I threw myself into work. A quick greeting for Mom—already hard at it in the kitchen—fast enough I could avoid inevitable questioning from the always intuitive Lucy Fleming, I focused all of my day on smothering my horrible state of mind and heart with the kind of business that required my absolute attention.

It worked, to a point. I was dirty, sweaty and only mildly grumpy by the time Daisy arrived at five to complete the interior decorations. Outside had been done weeks ago, Olivia's town initiative ensuring everyone had at least something festive to flaunt at their gate for the big night ahead. I'd put off the inside stuff until Daisy could give me a hand, though it had been out of the desire to spend a fun evening with her drinking wine and giggling over the task.

Yeah, likely not going to go the way I'd hoped, no fault of my bestie's.

She took one look at me and froze, her giant smile fading in a flash, big, expressive eyes flooding with concern as genuine as she was. Daisy dropped her bags of goodies at the door and hurried to me where I slumped in the middle of the foyer, unable to muster even a small grin.

She hugged me like I wasn't in serious need of a

shower before shaking me a little, that determined look on her stunning face that gave me a nervous feeling in the pit of my stomach.

"You," she said, "need a night out."

Well… maybe.

She hesitated a moment before shaking her head. "Listen, I know you're not a fan." Great way to start a conversation. "But." She beamed again, all enthusiasm returning in a brilliant flash that made me wince. Cranky? Check. Pessimistic naysayer? Check. Worst friend ever? Oh, checkity-check-check-check.

I know she saw my resistance, but Daisy was really good at getting what she wanted. Mostly by being completely kind and understanding and an excellent listener.

"What?" Benefit of the doubt. That was a step in the right direction.

"I'm going to a séance tonight," she gushed, rushing over my inevitable groan of denial. "It's going to be a blast. We can giggle over the utter patheticness of it all and go drink after." She winked, thick, dark lashes brushing her cheek as she did, white teeth flashing. How had she never decided to model? Then again, I would have hated for her amazingness to be tarnished by anything, including the fashion industry. "Just us girls."

I crossed my arms over my chest, stomach in knots all over again. "At Sadie's." Not a question. And utterly out of the question.

Her smile faded more slowly this time. "Fee, what happened?" She hesitated. "You're not okay, are you?"

I exhaled heavily, dropping my hands to my sides, shrugged. "I'm sorry, Day," I said, feeling on the edge of tears again and wishing I could just shake this funk I'd found myself in. Seriously, could I not get over myself already?

She steered me abruptly into the sitting room, planted me next to her on the sofa and stared into my eyes, hands holding mine. "You dump all of it right now," she said, crisp and no nonsense. "Hit me."

My lower lip trembled. This was stupid. "Day—"

"I meant right now, missy," she said. "No one hurts my Fee-Fee."

I choked out a laugh. Decided this was a terrible idea. Ended up unloading a bunch of sobbing, snotty, bitterness onto my best friend for the next ten minutes despite myself.

She nodded in the perfect places, made choice

comments that finally lured out a few giggles and hugged me hard when I was done. I snuffled, wiping my face and nose on the hem of my t-shirt, feeling better and leaning back into the cushions, faintly smiling at her while she fetched the box of tissues on the other side of the room before rejoining me.

"Thanks, Daisy," I said. "I have no idea what's wrong with me." I helped myself to a square and blew my nose. Gross, I hated crying.

My best friend squeezed my hand when I was done, her own expression soft and understanding. "I wish sometimes you could see yourself the way others see you," she said. "You're pretty awesome, Fee. That makes Vivian jealous. Robert, too. As for Sadie, she wants you to pay her to find your perfect mate." She rolled her eyes, laughed. "Crew, on the other hand…" Daisy shrugged at last, sitting back, staring out the window into the dark street like she didn't see it at all. "That man needs a prod in the ass. If you dating creates a solution either way, what's the harm?" She met my eyes again, hers serious. "Either you find someone you can love and who loves you like you deserve it, or you make him realize he's missing out on what he really wants and he'll do something about it."

So smart, my Daisy. Guess I was claiming a lot of people as mine lately.

"Now," she patted my knee with one hand before rising, beaming all over again, "let's get decorating so we have lots of time to drink wine before we head to the séance."

And that's how I found myself at Sadie Hatch's door two hours later, doing my best not to scowl, positive this was a terrible idea but unable to let Daisy down.

CHAPTER FIVE

I DON'T KNOW WHAT I was expecting. Hoodoo and a show, for sure, a bit of over-the-topness and a whole lot of you can't be serious. But I simply wasn't prepared for the level of commitment this woman went to in order to sell her shtick.

From the moment we set foot on her narrow cobbled walkway, the bushes looming toward us, untrimmed and spooky, I confirmed in my own mind I'd made a terrible choice coming here, Daisy downer or not. I mean, come on. How did Olivia let this crazy lady get away with such unkempt shrubbery when she called me out for an errant twig at every opportunity? I'd had to pull out the big arborist guns from the next town over when one of my maples leaned too far out over the street. Because tourists were all anti-twig, I guess. Pfft.

This place, though? Reeked of the kind of overdone with the intention of artful neglect one would likely expect to find in the house of a fortune teller. That was, if Hollywood designed the set. Maybe that's why Olivia wasn't standing at the foot of the walk right now, scowling at the looming foliage as if it offended her sensibilities.

So unfair. I should take up reading Tarot and see if that kept her away from my trees.

In any case, fake creepy with a dash of mwahaha was exactly the impression Sadie's gave me. Clearly, her choice of décor and personal dress was all tied into an elaborate front meant to add to the show. From the creaking old rocking chair that started up as we set foot on her dark porch, a single, dim bulb lighting the screen door, to the whispering of a distant voice as if piped in from a sound system just to give us goosebumps—it succeeded, if briefly—to the squeal inducing patter of the faintest touch of cobwebs that turned out to be a fine mist of water from an automated head above the door, she'd gone all out.

I convinced myself this was her Halloween persona. Not the real front for her business. Yeah, okay, sure. Except I was certain this whole dog and pony was her full time gig's normal.

I shivered despite myself inside my gold sweater, running my hands down the soft arms of the fluffy weave. The last time I'd worn this—the only time, actually—had been the day of the parade in April. The same day Skip Anderson died in my lap. I'd been saving it for a date with Crew, had stuffed it into the back of the closet after a brief laundering and a shudder. Somehow wearing it tonight fit not only my mood but was the perfect choice for a séance if I did say so myself. If Skip came back to haunt me, I'd have no one to blame but myself.

The door whipped open before my best friend could knock, the steady stare on the face of the old woman on the other side shutting me up more effectively than anything else ever had. Not that I was scared of her, not really. It was just the way she looked at me, like she knew everything about me. Again I decided this was about the worst life choice I could have made today of all days, still vulnerable from the hit she'd delivered yesterday, but I was out of options. Daisy had a firm grasp on my arm and was hauling me physically inside after her, past the watchful eyes of Sadie Hatch in her typical blindness inducing riot of colorful clothing. The woman needed a session with a paint chip pallet and a shrink.

"Welcome," she said in her grating voice, iron gray hair in a soft bun on the top of her head, riot of mix and match, I decided as I stepped past her, more than likely from utter lack of giving a crap what anyone thought. I could learn a thing from her after all, though the shrink thing was sounding more like my need than hers. "The others have gathered." She gestured into the house, the narrow entry bisected by a set of stairs heading upward and two doorways, one to a small sitting room on the left, the other into a large dining area on the right, with the hall leading deeper inside. I could hear chatter from the dining room and skirted Sadie, keeping my head down and letting Daisy lead the way into the room, breathing a faint sigh of relief we were past our host while my friend waved and chirped hello to the others.

I recognized the couple from yesterday at the party, the ones Sadie's grandson led her away to meet, saving me from more of her attention. Not that it helped. To my surprise, I found myself waving at Pamela Shard and her partner, Aundrea Wilkens, who both waved back, though the newswoman's rather embarrassed gesture had nothing on her girlfriend's enthusiasm.

Daisy was shaking hands with the couple and I caught their introductions as I copied her, happy to let her lead.

"Amos Cortez," the tall, wide-shouldered man said in a cultured voice. His dark hair had started to gray at the temples, full beard and mustache covering his strong features somewhat. But his handsome face seemed like he'd aged well, faint lines lending him gravity and a confident kind of attractiveness inside his gray suit. "My wife, Emelia."

I shook her hand too, murmuring the usual pleasantries as the woman offered her hand, her fingers trembling slightly. It was apparent from the redness of her own brown eyes, the puffiness of her thin face, that she'd been crying recently. Well, I knew how that felt, had taken a shower to do my best and wash away the ravages of my personal fit. It was pretty clear to me her hurt ran deeper than mine, that she was here at the séance likely to reach a lost loved one who touched her deeply. Really put my own mood in perspective.

I circled the table and accepted a hug from

Pamela, one from Aundrea. Both women had become good friends of mine since the murder of Aundrea's husband—a boon to her, it turned out—and they had finally been able to declare their love for each other. It was nice to see them both happy.

Way to trigger my funk all over again. And yet, they'd been forced to wait decades to be together. I had options. So my little downer nosedive could take a hike.

The other female guest seemed nervous as she hugged herself, a thin blue sweater tight around her as if to protect her from what was to come. A believer? Possibly, though her expression was unreadable past her seemingly anxious personal embrace. Beside her, his lined face settled into a deep and abiding scowl, sat Oliver Watters, our local historian. We'd met a few times, though never socially, in passing more than any real association. His books about Reading were a staple in most tourist places, his strong opinions making them more fiction than researched truth. I don't think I'd made a friend when he'd come to insist I carry copies in the foyer of Petunia's and turned him down.

Hey, I tried to be nice. Honest. Some people didn't like to take no for an answer and ended up slamming their way out my front door. Shrug.

I waved to both despite the fact Oliver's eyes tightened when he spotted me, not sure if the young woman was local or not, though she didn't look familiar.

"Alice," she said, unwinding enough to take her turn shaking my hand. She stared at me a long moment after she touched me before shaking her head, laughing a little, hazel eyes big behind her glasses. "Alice Moore."

"Fiona Fleming." I bobbed a nod, then tried a quick smile for Oliver. "Mr. Watters." Not that it was a requirement, but my parents raised me to be polite even if the old fart was a pompous ass. The old antique store owner and storyteller fit the profile.

He seemed to find my form of address flattering and preened a little in his tweed jacket, white hair in need of a trim wavering in thin, wisping strands around his ears. Crap. Did I just invite another visit from him with his box of books bent at the edges and that determined need he had to spread the Word of Oliver?

"Miss Fleming," he said, voice deep and gruff. "How's your father?"

Typical small town chatter. At least he kept his

confrontation with me quiet for now. Maybe he forgot I'd sent him packing? "Fine, thank you," I said. "I'll tell him you asked."

"Good man, Sheriff Fleming," he said. "Even with all the Malcolm Murray nonsense."

I stiffened, heart skipping a moment before I managed to inhale. The very Irish owner of The Orange, a local bar known for illegal poker games and what amounted to our very own mob right here in Reading (of all places) had alluded to the fact my father shared a history with him that I'd been at times eager and then fearful to discover. The fact that Oliver mentioned it in passing made me wonder if I was making too much of something that was common knowledge.

Before I could inquire, hands shaking a little as I drew a breath to ask, the final guest swept her way into the room in a waft of vanilla perfume and with a cold, blue stare that shut down my voice and my train of thought.

No. Not tonight of all nights, when I was still on edge and doing enough damage to myself without her being here. Anyone, I'd take anyone but Vivian French.

Guess that wasn't up to me.

CHAPTER SIX

DAISY. SHE HAD TO have known Vivian was going to be here. Except, when I glanced sideways at my best friend, the frown on her face told me she hadn't. Or that this was, at the very least, an irritating development.

I'd forgive her, then. Just as soon as I turned around and got myself out of there. Because no way was I hanging out for the evening with the woman who'd done everything she could yesterday to smear me into the ground under her teeny, pointed heel.

Before I could march myself to the door and back home for another dose of cake and likely a bottle of wine for a chaser, Daisy came to my side, hand on my elbow, a big smile on her face. "Don't let her see you flinch." How did she do that? She spoke so quietly I'm sure I was the only one who heard while her lips didn't even move.

Talented, if triggering. She was right, though. I could stomp my way home and let Vivian win. She would have to know my exit was due to her arrival. Could I give that victory to her after our encounter yesterday? Maybe if she hadn't been so horrible and her need to cut me down hadn't been so fresh, I might have shrugged off the fact I cared and made off for happier spaces. More likely, I wouldn't have been in a position to let her bother me at all. The best outcome, of course, was along the line of Daisy's suggestion. Show Vivian in no uncertain terms not one thing she said or did could get to me. Not now, not then, not ever.

In fact, the more I thought about it, sitting down, calm and composed and in control while she stewed over the fact I gave not one single crap about her or her little campaign to make me feel like I was nothing really was the only way to go.

Except, of course, that was the hardest choice, requiring the most strength. But I made it. And I upped the ante, pushing myself to not only show her I was fine but sat firmly down directly across from where she stood, next to Amos who shifted closer to his wife when I did. I ignored his reaction, instead focusing on Vivian who watched me with her mouth twisted into a bitter line. I crossed my arms over my chest and hoped I could make it through the next little while without lunging over the table at her.

Yes, that was better. There was my redheaded temper, my fiery refusal to be trod on like garbage. Screw her and the designer heels she strode in on. Her pathetic small girl tactics might work on others, but I was a Fleming and she was so transparent in her need to be better than me it was nothing short of laughable.

Take that, Vivs.

If she sensed the shift in me, she didn't show it, though she just as firmly sat, jerking the chair away from the table with the kind of squealing wood-on-wood that made me cringe, everyone falling silent while she took her seat, setting her expensive square of a handbag on the table, manicured nails in perfect ovals tapping the wooden surface in obvious agitation.

Huh, not like her to show emotion. Unless me being here was as much of a surprise to her as her arrival had been for me. Well, if that was the case, if my attendance shook Vivian from her miserable plans, I was happy to stay. Sure, fine. Maybe bitter resentment didn't look good on me, but I'd take it for now and feel badly about it later.

Just kidding. No way I'd feel bad over turning the uncomfortable tables on Vivian French.

"Are we going to do this or not?" She looked down at the expensive watch glittering on her wrist before she sat back, mimicking my move by crossing her arms over her narrow chest, her cream blouse wrinkling from the pressure of her unhappy clenching. The tiny gold cross on the thin chain around her neck surprised me. I'd never known her to be religious.

"Indeed." Sadie strode into the room with measured steps before turning and pulling on the tab of the pocket door she slowly, methodically slid closed, cutting us off from the rest of the house. When she spun back toward us she smiled, though it was a long, narrow smile, full of mystery and gave me a sense she observed us like a predator hunting a meal. "Welcome to my parlor and this evening of connection."

"Whatever," Oliver snapped, as grumpy on the outside as I felt on the inside, cutting through my own need to use bravado to lighten the mood. Daisy promised me this would be fun, that we'd laugh and drink wine and be silly. So far, her plan was sorely lacking in the any kind of amusement or alcohol department. "I'm here to see the show, nothing more. And to prove you're a fraud."

Huh. That was rather blunt. The look that passed between them had an edge to it, old hurt and anger on his side, disdain on hers. How well did these two know each other, then? I wasn't aware that Sadie might, in fact, be from Reading originally. Interesting.

Alice gently reached out, touched his arm and he grunted as if she'd spoken before falling still.

"Thank you for welcoming us," the young woman said, plain face reposed, unjudging. "I'm interested to see what's to come."

"I welcome unbelievers," Sadie said, a rather pointed glare passing between them, too, mostly from the old woman's side. "I have nothing to hide or to prove to those who have their own agenda." She gestured at the Cortez's who seemed startled to be singled out. "I am here to bring comfort and answers to those in need. Take from this experience what you will. The spirits will judge you where I will not."

Alice bowed her head to Sadie. "I'm only here to observe," she said.

Sadie didn't comment and Alice fell still, just watching as our host paced toward the far end of the table, taking a seat there. Alice showed no sign she didn't believe, aside from a careful scrutiny of Sadie while the woman settled into her own chair. Aundrea wiggled slightly on the psychic's right side, Pamela scowling at the tabletop. So she'd been dragged here, too, had she? I didn't miss the quick glare she shot at the old woman, though, nor the way her lips pursed like she wanted to say something. Even more interesting, with no time to comment or ask questions. That would have to come later. Because as soon as Sadie settled, the lights dimmed to murky near darkness.

Amos Cortez whispered something to his wife, Emelia sandwiched between him and Sadie, the tall man curving away from me, almost protectively around her as the room faded to dim illumination. Our host likely had controls we couldn't see, somewhere under the table. Typical chicanery and nothing to be impressed by. I settled in to absorb the performance while she spoke again. "The spirits come to those in need, but their messages are their own, and not always what we want or expect." She nodded slowly to the Cortez couple. Only Emelia nodded back, sniffing into a tissue.

"Whatever," Vivian snapped. "I only have an hour. If you could just get to it?" She glanced at me, then looked away as if she hadn't meant to. She looked like she wanted to just leave but, like me, was too stubborn to be the one to walk away. Interesting times three. What was she here for? I guess I'd find out.

It was clear, though, she wished I wasn't around. So there was no way I was leaving now.

"Very well," Sadie nodded to her, reaching for the tea set perched in the middle of the table. She slowly, carefully poured a cup, the aromatic blend I didn't recognize filling the room as she did. "This special tea allows me access to the spirit world. The chamomile, lavender, valerian root and cinnamon can aid the opening of intuition and cleanse blocks to reach across the veil to the other side."

Nice of her to share with the rest of us. Instead, we sat and watched her steep a cup in silence, muttering over it in a language I didn't recognize. Probably just made up words to add to the illusion of her power. She looked up, frowning, before gesturing to the middle of the table where a cream pot and a small bottle of honey with a fancy red label sat next to a plastic napkin dispenser shaped like a skull.

Alice moved faster than anyone else, sliding the tray with the goods toward Sadie who accepted with a grunt. It was hard not to sigh and tap my foot as she took her time opening the jar, finally twisting the cap off and helping herself, dipping her spoon in before stirring it in the steaming liquid as she spoke.

"There is a darkness here," she said, filling her cup to the brim with cream before tasting it, adding another dollop of honey. "Death lingers, the call of those whose loss has yet to be accepted by the echo they left behind." Emelia immediately began to cry, covering her mouth with more tissues her husband hastily provided. Who had she lost? And why did that description hit so hard? Sadie added yet another spoon load of the sweet stuff to the small cup, making my teeth ache. Why didn't she just drink the honey straight, for pity's sake? "Tonight, we open the way for those who choose to share their pain, their secrets, who long for release only we of the living can grant them. Eternal peace awaits if we are willing to allow them their rest."

Emelia hiccupped, sagged against her husband

who whispered something in her ear while Sadie licked her spoon and finally set it aside. Emelia shook her head at her husband and straightened, hands falling to her lap where she clasped the tissues tightly, a lifeline of some kind, and nodded.

"We're ready," she said in a small voice full of agony.

If her husband wasn't in the way I would have reached out to her, sitting so rigid and controlled like that. I knew what it felt like to hold in all those tears, though for different reasons. I almost did anyway, though the moment I decided to act, my hand just rising to extend past him to her, I felt something brush over my cheek.

It froze me in place. Felt it again a moment later while Daisy jumped beside me.

"What was that?" She met my eyes, her big ones wide, my sight adjusting to the low light enough I saw her shock clearly on her face.

"Come," Sadie said, setting aside her half-empty cup, voice deepening, commanding. "Come forth, those who have messages, those tortured souls who need our help. We are here. Come."

Wait, she hadn't lit any candles or set up props. No crystal ball, no anything. Just us, the tea set and that breeze. Okay, just wind, right? Some kind of machine, like the one outside that spit mist into my face. All a part of the act. I caught Alice frowning slightly and found myself watching her as things progressed.

And they did progress, pretty quickly, too. The breeze picked up, the faint sound of whistling joining the sudden flickering of the lights. Aundrea meeped in surprise, one hand over her mouth as she met my gaze with her own full of shock while someone whispered near my ear.

Okay, this was creepy and very cleverly done. Honestly, Sadie was very good at her job and I was actually starting to enjoy myself. Especially when, after a few seconds of the intensifying breath of air, the muttering voices, the lights trying to decide if they wanted to stay on or off, they died suddenly, plunging the room the rest of the way into total darkness.

CHAPTER SEVEN

WHAT FOLLOWED WAS THE most artful exploitation of the emotions and hearts of those around me I'd ever experienced. The faintest light returned, this time surrounding Sadie, forcing the eye to focus on her, keeping our attention from traveling anywhere around the room. A clever and subtle ploy that worked and worked very well, no bells and whistles required.

The moment the image of an older woman appeared behind Pamela, I knew Sadie Hatch had taken the art of soothsaying from a craft to utter perfection. The image didn't move, flickering much as the lights had, but when Pamela turned to look she squeaked like a mouse, shrinking sideways into Aundrea who held her tight while Sadie spoke.

"She's proud of you," she said, swaying softly, eyes closed, hands firmly pressed to the top of the table. So whatever she was doing had to be foot controlled. I needed to find out how she was doing it because this was theme park worthy, seriously. "No matter what you might think. And she wants you to be happy, Pamela."

My friend, my hard bitten reporter friend, actually burst into tears, glaring at Sadie with the kind of anger that made me nervous for her. But instead of speaking up about her rage, when Aundrea jabbed her in the ribs, Pamela started. "Thank you," she grunted while her partner hugged her.

Whatever that was. Okay then.

The image faded, Pamela turning back only to gasp and point toward me. I shifted abruptly at the sound of Daisy's name whispered near me, caught sight of her grandfather, Phil, smiling into the quiet darkness. Again he was still, utterly motionless, while Sadie spoke again.

"Daisy," she said. "He knows the accident wasn't your fault. You can release your guilt. He loves you still and waits for you on the other side."

Again I reminded myself this was meant to be funny, the pair of us finding humor in the event. Instead, there I sat, shocked to discover my beautiful friend blamed herself for the car crash that killed her grandfather when she was a kid, the same crash she survived. It happened so long ago I forgot about it, but apparently she hadn't. She cried into her hands, shoulders shaking as she nodded.

Um, holy crap. This was getting too serious for my liking. Far too real despite the fact I knew it had to be a con.

Phil's image vanished and Sadie paused, taking another drink of her tea. No one else moved or did the same, everyone staring at her while she shivered, sipped again, then set her cup aside and bowed her head just as the next spirit appeared.

This time behind Aundrea. Pete's grim and hideous smile made my stomach crawl, and to my surprise, Aundrea seemed emotional at his appearance.

"He's a different man on the other side," Sadie said, "and he wishes you happiness, Aundrea. His regret holds him here. Do you forgive him for the harm he caused?"

How could she? He trapped her in marriage,

blackmailed her into staying with him in collusion with her horrible family. No way would—

"Yes," she whispered, loud and clear. Blinked at his still form hovering there, glowing faintly. "Of course I forgive you." She squeezed Pamela's hand and they smiled at each other though Pamela's was strained.

Only then did I understand. This hadn't been a visit intended for Pamela. It was the means for Aundrea to find forgiveness. Nor was it to help Pete in the afterlife. He was long dead and I was very much positive he'd gone somewhere he was suffering if karma actually existed. This was, instead, an effort to heal Aundrea. That I could accept. Besides, it wasn't like Pete was really here. I silently shook myself, reminded this was just a hoax, a show.

Still. This was way cooler than I'd been expecting and I actually caught myself grinning and swept up in the fun of it at last. Couldn't wait to get home and gossip with Daisy about the spectacle the old woman came up with.

Vivian twitched when Pete disappeared, as if anticipating the spirit that appeared behind her. She didn't turn around, rigid and cold, not a hint of emotion showing while the sweet-faced boy blinked into view. He looked like her, but she didn't have kids.

"Vivian," Sadie said, her tone rising faintly, the echo of a child's tone coming through. "You couldn't have known, that day at the lake. It was the bee sting that killed him, not falling in the water."

She flinched ever so faintly. "I know that already," she snapped.

"And yet, you refuse to accept it," Sadie said, droning and stern. "Your guilt haunts you. Your brother never blamed you." She shook faintly, one hand rising to touch her face, fingers trembling as her "channeling" took her strength or something equally trite.

Brother? Wait, Vivian had a brother?

"Whatever," she sat back in her chair, the image of the boy flickering out. "This is stupid." She looked away, jaw working, before her head snapped around again. "I wanted to talk to my aunt." She glared at Sadie, frustration obvious. "You said you could do that." Her quick look my way made it clear she knew she sounded ridiculous. She tsked then, tapping her fingernails on the table. "I need to know where she filed that paperwork."

So, two Vivian points to ponder. A deceased

brother I knew nothing about and some kind of lost files? While the death of her sibling wasn't something to be amused by—and I wasn't—knowing Vivian didn't care about his passing as much as she did some stupid papers confirmed everything I thought about her and more.

A tiny, nasty, evil part of me hoped she never found what she was looking for. Sigh. That was going to fester.

The boy gone, Sadie sagged slightly before opening her eyes again, sipping tea, meeting Vivian's. "I don't get to choose who crosses," she said. Her words came slightly slurred, cheeks pink as the teacup rattled on the saucer. Wow, she really committed to her act, didn't she?

Vivian snarled briefly before looking away, glaring with irritation into the darkness. But I noticed she didn't go and I soon found out why.

"Patience," Sadie said, steadying herself. "Stay after and we'll try again in a private session."

Ah, the money grab. Gotcha.

I felt a shiver climb down my spine the instant the glow appeared in my peripheral vision. Behind me. The same moment a woman's voice whispered my name in my ear. I turned slowly, forcing myself to stay calm, knowing what I'd see and unsurprised to find Grandmother Iris standing behind me. Wait, I knew that image, a photograph I had of her. I'd already known this was a sham, but well done, bravo, standing ovation and all that.

"Fiona," Sadie said. "She's so grateful you said yes. That you care so deeply for the home she made for herself and her guests. And that you have taken on her role."

Uh-huh. "Thanks," I said, staring right at the fortune teller, deciding to have a little fun after all. "For the music box."

No way she could know about it, not if this wasn't really my grandmother. I was rewarded with a twitch from Sadie whose eyes opened briefly before she snapped them shut again.

"A token of her love, to remind you of her always," she said. She was smooth, I'd give her that. Not a hint of frustration or curiosity, though the vibration in her voice was back, the shake of her hand as she dug deep for her part. Faker. She just succeeded in telling me she was likely prescreening us and used the time before our arrival to pull enough detail from the internet and social media to convince those who wanted to be convinced.

No map, no doubloon. Not my grandmother. Oddly, I was disappointed.

Iris disappeared rather abruptly while I settled into my seat more firmly, exhaling out the last of my bad humor. At least Sadie had finished the circle she'd started, leading me back to amusement. Enough I winked at Daisy who winked back, faint smile showing me she knew better, too, despite her earlier tears.

"What, nothing for me?" Oliver spat the words out while Sadie sipped her tea once more, emptying it. The cup thudded to the saucer as she drew a breath, seemed to hesitate, then spoke.

She smiled at him, mild but cool, face now pale as death. "If you'd allow it," she said. "But your spirit blocks any attempt the souls of those who love you make to reach you." She sniffed softly, head bobbing before she caught herself. "A shame, but truth."

"And me?" Alice seemed about as composed as our hostess, still, quiet.

Sadie's shoulders rolled forward, her expression kind before she flinched, one hand pressing to her chest. "Nothing so far, my dear," she said, now frowning and a bit breathless. "Not that I would think you need me to communicate with the dead."

What did that mean exactly? "But allow me to continue."

Alice flinched from the comment but didn't respond as Sadie resumed her position. This time her head bowed, her face scrunching as she seemed to be caught in some kind of otherworldly grasp. She moaned briefly, the wind picking up, ruffling my hair, the whispering increasing, layering over with multiple voices until I shivered despite myself.

Everything fell suddenly still, punctuated by the choking half-sob that escaped Emelia as if she knew exactly what was coming.

"He's here," Sadie said. "Manuel is with us." She moaned again, deeper this time, falling forward, catching herself from face planting the table with both hands.

Emelia spun to look, but no one appeared this time. "Where? Where is my son?"

Ah, question answered. Amos looked around, clearly anxious, though he was more focused on his wife, it seemed, than any possibility his dead child might appear. So she was the believer, clear enough.

"He can't cross," Sadie wailed. "The mysterious illness that took his life anchors him still to this plane, but it smothers him on the other side, keeping him from our sight."

"No!" Emelia's denial was like a knife blade to the heart. So much pain. For the first time, I felt deep animosity toward Sadie. Yes, she'd insulted me yesterday, but that was minor compared to the clearly horrendous damage she'd done to this woman, offering her fake insights in her fraudulent game. "Please, I have to speak to him. He has to tell me what happened, what killed him." She started sobbing again, whole body trembling. "Please. My poor baby."

I was pretty much done at this point. I turned to tell Sadie to stop, ready to turn the lights on myself if I had to, when Alice gasped suddenly and the entire room fell silent.

It was almost as if someone wrapped the room in a cold hand, chill in the air triggering goosebumps on my skin. I caught motion in the corner of my eye, turned in time to see a glowing, ghostly figure float through the pocket door and come to a halt at the far end of the table. This time, rather than a static image, the young man raised both arms, eyes black pits of emptiness, mouth gaping open as he reached for Emelia.

Who screamed and reached back. "Manuel!"

I'd be nominating Sadie for an Oscar for this performance. Right after my terror at this new and utterly believable trick allowed me to breathe.

Manuel Cortez's face contorted, his expression flashing to utter rage before he exploded into a million pieces of bright light. I claim zero embarrassment that I screamed like a little girl along with the rest of the group, the rush of adrenaline as blackness plunged the room into pitch darkness making it impossible to see thanks to the bright light aftereffect of the exploding ghost.

Yup, best show in town. She really needed to charge a premium for this.

I finally got my heart going again, laughed shakily into the dark, grasped for Daisy's hand. "Holy," I whispered.

She giggled next to me. "I know, right?" Paused. "Um, Sadie?"

Was there more to the show?

"I think something's wrong." That was Alice. The sound of a chair moving made me jump. "Sorry." Alice again. "I think the lights are here." Sudden brightness lit the room in a blaze of illumination, so much so I flinched from the assault, blinking a few times before I could see around me.

And stared, stunned and more than a little creeped out, into the empty, vacant eyes of a very dead Sadie Hatch, the most terrified look on her face I'd ever seen.

CHAPTER EIGHT

THE SOFT SOUND OF Crew's deep voice should have made me feel better. Would have, I guess, if it hadn't been for the resigned look on his face when he'd walked into the house, saw me there, shook his head. Because this was becoming a habit I really, really wished I could break.

Not my fault people died around me. It was just bad luck, wrong place, wrong time. And I wasn't alone, either, right? There was a room full of people who'd been here when Sadie met her end. That definitely didn't mean I was cursed or anything.

Was I?

He didn't say anything to me, his handsome face

composed and professional, the faint hint of a beard on his square jaw, well past the end of the day for him though he looked comfortable and confident in his beige button up and jeans, dark hair just past the point he needed a trim to keep it perfect. Not that I minded a bit of untidiness. In fact, I would have loved to push it back from his forehead with one hand, feel the silky heaviness of it against my skin. The heat of him near me. The scent of him, coffee and vanilla and other sweetly dark and delicious things that had a bit of an effect on my senses I struggled to control.

Oh, Fee. I was so screwed.

Why did I retreat, head down, feeling embarrassed by my presence here when there wasn't anything I could do about it? Of course, the vulnerability I still fought with came back all over again, doubt miring me in worry he'd find more reason not to be with me thanks to this recurring issue I had with dead bodies.

Issue. Yeah, that's what it was. Just a bit of a problem, nothing serious. It was only murder.

Maybe murder. There was nothing saying she'd died of anything but natural causes, actually. No blood, no sign of strangulation, no frothing at the

Patti Larsen

mouth indicating poison. And yes, okay, so I'd done enough research and spent enough time as the daughter of a sheriff I could spot typical signs of foul play. The timing had to be more than a coincidence. No way the old woman had a heart attack or a sudden catastrophic stroke or aneurysm the very moment her crowning achievement—the most realistic ghost apparition I'd ever dreamed I'd see— made his debut.

As much as the detective in me wanted to know more details, I instead found myself herded with everyone else into the small parlor on the other side of the entry, while deputies Jillian Wagner and my hateful cousin Robert stood guard.

Maybe I could have convinced my cop friend to let me through. But with Robert there, no way was Jill going to step out of line. Robert had too much fun making trouble for others to put her job at risk like that. I didn't blame her and, quite frankly, I was happy to sit there and wait my turn, to keep my head down and pretend like I had nothing to do with this.

Wait, pretend? I didn't. I hadn't killed the old woman. I was just here for fun with my bestie. Damn it, why did I feel so guilty then?

Amos appeared at the door, rejoining his wife

70

who wept on the sofa, Daisy kindly sitting with her until her husband returned. Crew stood in the entry, eyes landing on me and he sighed, gestured.

"Fiona," he said in a resigned tone of voice. "You're next."

Vivian jerked to her feet, glaring between me and him like this was some kind of conspiracy. "I have to go, Crew," she said. "I can't sit here all night like this."

"I'll be right with you," he said, mild enough I knew that he was on the edge of losing his temper. Any second now that vein in his forehead would appear and the tic on his cheek, just below his blue eye, would start jumping. Except, of course, while Vivian triggered it, I'd be the one who got to set it off and see it evolve.

Awesome. Lucky me.

I stood and went quietly, not a peep, hoping to get this over with quickly. Even while the part of me that hated being told what to do, the big girl who could take care of herself and why was I being an idiot like this, shouted at me to get a backbone already.

Crew stepped past me as Jill and Robert closed ranks at the door, blocking my view of the others.

The sheriff gestured for me to sit on the steps. I did so, well below his eye line as he leaned against the bannister, one booted foot on the first tread, his expression calm enough, though the tightness around his eyes was far too familiar.

"Okay, Fee," he said, long suffering. "What happened this time?"

I think it was Robert's snigger that set me off. Maybe it was the utter unfairness of all of this, of my proximity to death that was never my fault. Or perhaps it was a final blow, a lit end of a fuse started yesterday when the dead woman insulted me to the quick follow up blow after blow to my self-esteem. I don't know what finally made me snap out of my funk, but I was grateful.

And royally pissed off.

"You think I do this on purpose?" I shot that at him with enough venom he started, eyes wide. Even Jill and Robert looked shocked, the smirk wiped from my cousin's face. "You think I wander around Reading looking for people to die on me, Crew? Seriously?" I had to force myself to pull back, to glare when I would have liked to just get up and storm out, slamming the door as hard as I could behind me. "Screw you and the ugly boots you walked in on."

Crew swallowed carefully while Jill's lips twitched. She looked away, fighting laughter, but I didn't care if she thought it was funny. I was done being blamed by him for things that were so far out of my control it made me crazy.

"I'm sorry," he said then, contrite enough I felt my temper settle to a stewing bubble. I wasn't letting it go yet. "You just have... unusual luck."

"It's a small town," I snapped. "And I'll remind you I was far from the only person here."

Or at Skip's death in the parade in April. Or at Mason Patterson's at the White Valley Ski Lodge last Valentine's Day. And as for Pete Wilkins, he might have died in my koi pond, but he'd had help a long time before I found him.

So there, Sheriff Smartass.

Crew nodded, seemed to realize he was never going to win this battle, and forced a smile past the snap in his blue eyes. No way did he get to be mad at me. "Let's start again," he said. "Can you tell me what happened?"

I unfolded the evening to him as I remembered it, as quickly and yet thoroughly as I could. Impossible not to, considering the father I'd been raised with.

Dad taught me to pay attention to detail, if not to be a cop myself. Though I wondered if he knew just how much he'd rubbed off on me already when he told me in no uncertain terms he didn't want me to follow in his footsteps.

Still rankled.

By the time I finished, shivering just slightly at the memory of the final apparition before the light died, I was much calmer. Robert's grin was back and he snorted when I described Manuel's transformation from glowing, hovering ghost to vengeful looking spirit that exploded into light.

"You're always such a drama queen, Fanny," he said.

Crew's scowl shut up my cousin quickly and I wondered just how much of the sheriff's impatience came from this murder and what percentage was fed by having to put up with that idiot every day.

If I had to work with Robert, I'd end up shooting him.

Crew was turning back to me, more questions to ask, obviously, when the door slammed open and the young man who'd lured Sadie away at the party yesterday came through, hands grasping two full white plastic bags which he promptly dropped, shock on his face.

"What's going on?" He looked around, a bit of desperation in his eyes, voice squeaking just faintly. Jill cut him off when he tried to move further into the house, a gentle but firm hand on his chest.

"And you are?" Crew's kind tone was reserved for others, apparently. I glared at him while he joined his deputy, both hands held up to keep the young man from bolting.

"Denver Hatch," he said in a quavering voice, eyes locked on the dining room door. "Where's my grandmother?"

Crew didn't answer, asking a question of his own. "Where have you been, Denver?" He looked down into the bags the young man dropped. "Shopping this late?"

"Halloween treats." Denver swallowed, prominent Adam's apple bobbing, clipped black fuzz of hair already thinning. His skinny frame trembled, one hand wiping over his mouth as he met Crew's eyes. "Is she...?"

Another intrusion, the door gently bumping Denver in the back as Dr. Aberstock finally arrived, cutting off the question. The portly, white-bearded local physician smiled and waved at me, the hem of his cape catching in the door as it swung shut behind him. He sighed and flipped it loose, but not before exposing the full-on, screen worthy vampire costume that adorned him, from crimson sash and cravat to giant gold necklace to the tuxedo he wore under that red-lined cape. Charming. Though oddly creepy, considering he looked enough like Santa Claus that the twist in his costume choice took on a decidedly eerie bent. Or maybe it was just me.

"Doc." Crew nodded quickly, gestured toward the dining room. The doctor smiled professionally in response and headed for the body while Denver crumpled a bit, Jill catching him before he fell.

"I was right," he whispered. "I knew something happened to her. I just knew it. She's dead, isn't she?"

Crew guided Denver toward the sitting room, Jill and Robert turning with him. Leaving me three options. Number one, I could head for the front door. It was right there, unguarded, unmanned. Hoof it for home and lock the door and forget this happened, that I was part of yet another death and another investigation. That meant leaving Daisy behind, though, and I couldn't do it, abandon her for my own preservation.

Option two, I could be a good little girl and go back into the sitting room, join the others. Sit, wait, answer more questions, because Crew loved his questions, and finally go home when he released all of us at once.

My third option beckoned with the kind of luring siren song that ended in tears and shouting, the sort of horrible decision making impulse that led me from disaster to disaster on a regular enough basis I really did need to talk to a therapist. Didn't do a thing to stop me from turning to stare at the pocket door left open just a crack when Dr. Aberstock slid it shut behind him.

I was in exactly the right—wrong?—frame of mind to take Door #3. With bells on.

Before I knew I was moving I was up, across the entry and sliding the door open, tucking it closed behind me.

CHAPTER NINE

D
R. ABERSTOCK DIDN'T SEEM surprised to find me invading his space. If anything, he accepted my appearance with the kind of happy welcome that I'd seen him reserve for Dad and even Crew at crime scenes. I could take that as a compliment or the twisted truth I really did poke my nose in too often. Guess which one I beat myself with?

"Another day, another body, right, Fee?" He bent over his case, cape and jacket discarded, gloves on his hands, grunting softly as he pulled on a disposable white suit over his tuxedo. I ran to help when the hood got caught in his suspenders and he winked his gratitude. "Stupid protocols," he said. "I get it, but

Crew's a bit of a stickler these days, more so than he's ever been." He shook his head, hood covering his hair, making him look like a round, squishy marshmallow with blood running from one corner of his beard and the black makeup he'd applied rather a ghastly counterpoint. "Gloves?"

I glanced down into his kit, noting the blue box and grinned despite myself. No, this wasn't fun. No, I shouldn't be here. Yes, I was going to snoop because, well. Crew was going to yell at me anyway when he found me here. Might as well earn it. "Thanks."

Thirty seconds later I cruised the room, keeping my hands to myself despite the gloves I now wore, half observing Dr. Aberstock as he did his investigation. I heard the door to the house open, knew the paramedics would be here any second, and took a chance to ask a question, though not the one I'm sure he was expecting.

"Dracula, really?"

He laughed, shrugged. "My wife's idea," he said. "Trust me, not my first choice. But according to Bernice, one cannot go as a mad scientist to a Patterson family party."

Pattersons, huh? The founding family, of which

Aundrea was a member, had been a mysterious and influential part of Reading since the good Captain founded our fair town, bringing his sidekick of a cabin boy with him. Joseph Patterson's progeny remained, while the pirate's didn't, oddly. "Funny Aundrea wasn't there?"

The doctor paused a moment while the pocket doors slid open and two young women in medic uniforms—neither of whom I recognized—nodded to us as they entered. Likely dispatched from another town.

"Now that you mention it," Dr. Aberstock said. And then gestured to the paramedics, forgetting to finish, I guess.

Hmmm. Well, it was no secret Aundrea was on the outs with her family, considering her choice to out her relationship with Pamela, something her own father had done everything he could—including recruiting Pete to blackmail her—to keep her from exposing to the world. And yet, she had a controlling share in their matters, through her son, Jared. Weird that she'd choose to come here tonight instead of a family do.

None of my business. I shook off the question, feeling a bit guilty over being nosy about my friend's affairs. And instead continued my poking about more immediate concerns. Snooping priorities, yo.

It was quickly apparent Sadie's setup was far more sophisticated than anything I'd encountered before, and not just from experiencing it. There was no sign of any wires, nothing to indicate any kind of traditional controls like the one's I'd seen in other operations like this one. There was a time in New York I loved going to stuff like this, just like Daisy suggested, if only to have a good laugh. Easy enough to spot the fakery for the most part, though my tour around the room—careful not to touch a thing—showed me nothing obvious.

Dr. Aberstock backed away from Sadie and the paramedics took over, sliding the chair slowly back so he could get a good look before loading her carefully onto a stretcher. Crew and his deputies had spent some time in here, so I could only assume all of the evidence collection and photos had already been handled. But I wanted to be sure there was absolutely no way I could mess up the sheriff's investigation.

"Hard to tell if it was natural causes or not," Dr. Aberstock said, shedding his white suit and stuffing it into his case while he spoke. "I'll take a closer look when I get to the morgue. For now, it looks like some kind of heart attack, but that could have been caused by a foreign influence."

Good to know. Made me pause and consider. She'd been acting funny, shaking, seemed in distress from time to time. Part of the show, as I'd first assumed, or some symptom of impending death? But would she ignore it if she wasn't well in favor of the con? "Thank you," I said.

He laughed then, tossing his cape and coat over one arm, case in the other hand. Time for his own unexpected question. "Why aren't you on the force, Fee?"

Surprise melted into hesitation before I smiled weakly back. "I'm just a B&B owner, Doc."

He shook his head at me, shrugged. "Tell Crew I'll have a report for him in the morning, though toxicology could be a bit. The lab's backed up." He left then, whistling softly to himself, while I watched him go, heart clenched for an old reason that had nothing to do with murder. And yet, everything to do with it.

Why *wasn't* I a cop? Because my father insisted I pursue anything but law enforcement and though he'd recently changed his mind on that idea, it was far too late for me now.

Right?

Crew's voice echoed from the entry and, in my haste to finish my snooping, I ducked beside Sadie's chair, peeking at the floor. That move finally put me in a position to uncover some evidence of her fraud. A small panel, digital and highly sophisticated, had been screwed into the facing board of the table. Wireless, from the lack of connections giving it away. Subtle enough to be missed by the casual observer, but the glass screen was covered in fingerprints.

Wait, she'd had her hands on the table the whole time, right? Crew's voice came closer, angry now. Did he just say my name? Whoops. But no, when she stopped to drink tea, her right hand held the cup. While her left disappeared.

So, this was an elaborate setup all right. Preprogrammed somehow? Interesting. I would never expect someone like Sadie to—

Oh. Of course. The grandson. How clever.

"So that's how she did it."

I just managed to suppress a squeal of terror, falling on my butt and clutching at my chest in fright. Alice's face flashed with surprise and then remorse as she grasped for me, pulling me up again, shaking her head with a weak laugh.

"I'm so sorry," she said. "I didn't even consider the timing."

I grasped her hand a moment, my own shaky laughter breathless but the kind of release I needed right now. "You're very good at sneaking," I said. Crew's angry tone increased in the hall outside the door.

She glanced that way, grinned at me. "You, too," she said. "The paramedics were a good distraction." She frowned and gestured at the panel. "Clever."

"Tell me about it." I rubbed my arms with both hands to shed some of the adrenaline she'd sent surging through me. Yes, this was a terrible idea, but I admitted I was happiest with a mystery to solve. "Even more so how she saved the best for last. Lulled us with the stillness of the images and then bam!"

Alice looked uncomfortable a moment, like she was going to say something before smiling faintly. "Right."

So there was more to it? "You disagree?" Wow, Crew was really working himself into pissed off out there. I heard, "Fiona," and, "home?" and, "better NOT be," as Alice spoke.

"I'm sure you're right," she said. "It's just..."

Just. That the last ghost, the image of Manuel... how did Sadie do it? Two minutes alone with Denver and I'd have my answers, I was positive of it.

I stood, grinning to myself, just as Crew strode through the door. Probably the worst expression I could have been wearing at that moment. At least, that was the impression he gave me from the instantaneous flushing of deep scarlet that overcame his cheeks and how his angry tic leaped into almost immediate evidence.

He didn't have to say anything. I knew I was in trouble, had known the moment I decided to take this route, to sneak into his domain and do my own digging. I just couldn't muster regret and I'm sure it showed on my face as much as my rather challenging grin had. In fact, I held up both hands with a sheepish smile, showing him I at least made sure not to tamper.

"Dr. Aberstock said he'll have a report for you tomorrow." Yeah, that was helping.

Crew's blue eyes narrowed to slits as he spun his body sideways and pointed with trembling aggression at the door. "Fiona Fleming. *Out.*"

I complied, peeling off the latex, tucking them

into my pocket, this close to asking him why he hadn't given the same order to my companion but managing to save myself from that smartass comment with a swift internal pinch. Alice eased past him, keeping her head down, not needing to be told, I guess. I should have mimicked her, acted contrite even if I didn't feel it one bit. But there was something in the air tonight, a giddy sense of self I'd been missing since Sadie's comment the day before—hell, if I was going to be honest, since I left Reading angry and confused because I couldn't live the life I wanted thanks to Dad—that swept over me. This rollercoaster of emotion had to stop. I hoped it stopped right freaking here.

I held Crew's eyes on the way out, knowing I was still grinning, cheeks aching from it, a giggle bubbling in my stomach. I wasn't complaining about the release or the freedom it stirred inside me, but what was wrong with me, really? I'd flipped over from horribly lonely and down on myself to a giddy excitement I shouldn't be feeling in the face of the death of another person. I handed Crew the gloves on the way by before striding with the kind of confidence I normally noted as Daisy's day-to-day charismatic strut out of the dining room, taking my best friend's hand on the way through. Easy to ignore Vivian's glare, the questioning eyebrow raise from Jill, how Robert scowled as if I'd kicked him and swept from the house, the queen of the world.

Time to face facts and accept I was happiest when I had a mystery to solve.

CHAPTER TEN

THE GIDDY HIGH LEFT me by the time I hit the sidewalk, though regret didn't show up. Daisy tugged hard on my hand, laughing as she cast a look over her shoulder, the sound of voices behind me—I refused to look back—telling me Crew let everyone go for now. Because there'd be more questions, endless questions, his typical way of doing business. For the moment, I was happy to breathe night air and embrace how I was feeling.

"You're in so much trouble." Daisy's eyes glittered with amusement.

"Whatever," I said, brushing it off, loving my reclaiming of myself as the crisp evening air washed away the last of my gloom. Screw it. Screw it all.

"Not like I haven't been in the middle of this stuff before. He should be used to it by now."

My best friend snorted. "Find anything good?"

I filled her in on what I'd discovered, the easing of my bubbling joy doing nothing to ruin my mood. In fact, by the time we landed on the doorstep at Petunia's, I felt the most calm and collected I ever had. Ever. So weird, like the whole world was utterly clear and I knew exactly who I was, why I was here. Not specifics, just that sort of awakening that I'd always heard about but never got to experience before.

I hoped I could make it last.

Mom and Dad stood in the foyer when I opened the door, both of them pale and staring as we entered. I stopped in my tracks, taking in their matching costumes, my father dressed as some kind of old world P.I. and Mom in a 40's suit and pillbox hat that made her look like a silver screen star.

"Fee!" Mom came to me, my pug following her as she hugged me. "Are you okay, sweetie?"

I hugged her back, then Dad when he joined us, Daisy accepting her own embraces while Petunia sat at our feet and panted her joy we were home.

"We're fine, Mom," I said. Rolled my eyes at

Dad. "Don't say it." Because it was pending, his judgement.

Except instead of giving me the hard time I was expecting, Dad shook his head, frowning. "I'm not saying anything. I'm glad you're okay."

"It was horrible and creepy and unforgettable." I let Daisy spill everything as we all sat in the front room and she unfolded our night. Much more eloquently than I could have with enough storytelling ability Mom was gasping and reacting like this was some kind of radio play. Okay, maybe her outfit wasn't helping the imagery I built in my head, but Dad's silence and careful listening was about as character specific as he could get.

Any second now he'd drawl out a trite line and call my friend dollface for good measure.

"How did you two find out about this?" I waited until Daisy drew a breath, her eyes on me, about to spill my act of rebellion—she was at that point in the story, so it had to be her next statement. Instead, knowing Dad might react badly to my snooping, I deflected. He'd find out soon enough anyway, but I wanted my own answers first. And to sit in this supportive circle a little while longer.

"We were at the party with Lloyd and Bernice

Aberstock when Crew called," Mom said, turning to meet Dad's eyes. "Olivia was having a fit, as usual. When we found out you were there, we came right home."

"Crew cut his interrogation routine short for once?" Dad's sarcasm wasn't lost on me. They had such different approaches to investigation that it was no wonder they butted heads over cases. Right, because that head butting had nothing to do with the fact Dad liked to interfere about as much as his daughter did. Now that he was retired, Dad wasn't supposed to be involved anymore either. Like that was going to stop him.

"I'm assuming I pissed him off to the point he couldn't think, so he sent us home." I sighed then and confessed what I'd found while Dad chuckled.

"You know how to push his buttons," he said.

That was it? "You're not going to tell me to say out of it?" He'd confessed he knew I should have been a cop but was worried about me and the life it would mean for me. But he was usually with Crew on the side of mind my own business.

Dad sighed, leaning back into his chair, eyes locked on me. "Kiddo," he said, "I've realized telling you or your mother what to do is such a colossal waste of time I might as well save my breath. Besides," he grinned slowly, "you're pretty good at this. Tweaking Crew's nose can't hurt him. He's too bound by his training sometimes. Maybe a dose of Fiona Fleming now and then is what he needs to make his own rules."

And maybe a bit of John Fleming for good measure? Dad was so transparent, I could see his mental cogs turning and if I didn't know him as well as I did I would have missed the glee under his tone.

Mom smacked Dad's knee. "Fee," she said, "your father is right and wrong in so many ways." She then shook her index finger at me. Adorable. "If he won't say it, I will."

I grinned openly then. "Stay out of it!" Dad, Daisy, me, all in a chorus that was far too full of humor for the situation but made my best friend giggle anyway.

Mom's lips twitched, her nostrils flaring in annoyance. And then she laughed.

"Is Olivia okay?" I broke the moment with that question. "The last thing she needs is another murder." Come to think of it, we'd had a rough go as a town the past sixteen months. Crew might point fingers at me being around when the deaths

GHOSTS AND GOBLINS AND MURDER

happened, but it wasn't lost on me the increase in tourism meant this increase in crime, too. Surely that had to weigh on Olivia's mind?

Mom glanced at Dad again, Daisy making a soft, sad sound.

"I don't know," Mom said. "I don't think so. She's struggling, Fee."

Dad's hard shell softened as he nodded. "Pretty sure she's on her way out as our mayor," he said. "Damned shame. She's done so much for us. While I don't agree with all of her tactics, she's put so much pressure on herself she's starting to crack."

"The council is so cruel to her," Mom said, cheeks pink. "No gratitude for all her hard work." Now, my mother had her moments standing up to Olivia, when it was required. But her empathy was all Lucy Fleming. "Since Skip's death it seems like there's been one disaster after another. The pirate debacle, for instance."

Dad snorted. "She had to go that way. Just had to." He sighed deeply. "There's a couple of treasure hunters publically debunking the whole thing, making her the laughingstock. Us as a town, too. Not to mention Skip's very public murder."

While the death of the football player was old

news, I had no idea about the debunkers. That could really put a dampener on tourism. Or it could increase it, since all press was good press, right? I briefly considered telling them about the map piece his mother left me, the doubloon, exchanged a quick look with Daisy to that effect. But Mom glared at Dad, cutting him off, and spoke.

"It's not just that," Mom said like he blamed Olivia for her choice of marketing. "The Lodge had issues all summer with things going wrong." I knew that from personal experience. I'd heard the complaints, had to field calls from angry customers looking for somewhere else to stay with nowhere to put them. "Jared's done his best to step up where his father failed, but there's only so much he can accomplish." Pete's frauds and building code violations had happened right in the middle of the Lodge's construction. I could only imagine how much it would take to fix his mess. I liked Jared a lot, but I didn't envy him what he was up against. "I wish there was a way to help her. But I agree with John. She's likely going to lose the next election. And I'm not sure there's anyone who can do her job as well as she's done it."

I had some ideas about that, namely the redhead

in the prim suit and hat sitting in front of me, but then again I wouldn't wish the pressure that Olivia bore on my mother, so I let it go.

"John," Daisy said, "how much do you know about Sadie?"

He didn't get to answer. The front bell rang, startling me, all of us. Daisy squeaked, laughed softly at her response. I rose before she could—her reaction was out of habit, I guess—and headed for the door, mind whirling, Petunia padding at my feet.

When I opened it, all of my thoughts stopped, stilled. Emelia and Amos Cortez stepped through without preamble, dragging carryon bags rolling behind them.

"Oh, it's you!" The grieving mother hugged me, her embrace trembling still. "What a relief." That was an odd thing to say? She glanced at her husband, who nodded his agreement. "We're in need of a room, if you have one available."

CHAPTER ELEVEN

D AISY RUSHED TO HELP as I checked the couple in, Dad appearing to carry their bags upstairs for them while Emelia sagged against her husband when he gave me their information in a dull, tired voice. When he fumbled and dropped his credit card, Petunia rushing forward to sniff it just in case it was food, he frowned and swore softly in Spanish before wincing at me. Daisy quickly retrieved the card, handing it to me with a soft pat for the disappointed pug, while Emelia crouched to scratch Petunia's ears with a tiny smile on her face.

"Sorry," Amos muttered. "It's been a long day and we're both worn out." He looked down at his wife, face expressionless. "A long six months." He met my eyes then, his deep brown ones lined with old sorrow. "The sheriff told us this was the closest place to stay. Thanks for taking us on short notice."

"My pleasure," I said. Winced at the terminology. But he waved off my expression.

"We're actually happy it's you," he said, repeating his wife's comment before expanding on it. "Means fewer questions to answer." Ah, that made total sense when I thought about it. They had to be just as tired of people inquiring about their situation, added to the weight of the death tonight. I know I would be, was of the not-so-subtle proddings about my real reasons for leaving New York. I'd just left a cheating boyfriend behind, by choice. They'd lost their son from what sounded like suspicious circumstances they had no answers for.

Daisy led them upstairs, key in hand, while I finished off their booking. Mom joined me, guiding me to the kitchen, her pillbox hat in her hand, suit coat unbuttoned. It wasn't long before a pot of tea sat between us, the only light the small bulb over the stove making shadows in the large room, and though I hesitated over caffeine this late I accepted a cup, not ready for bed yet, knowing I'd be tossing and turning if I did try to sleep.

"Something's up with you tonight." Mom's face scrunched, nose wrinkling in that adorable way of hers. "Sorry, I know. Someone died. I'm being terribly unkind. But it's not that." She shifted on the stool, heels of her shoes hooked in the dividers on her seat. Her head cocked to one side, a smile growing on her face. "You've been so down lately. It's nice to see that's lifted."

Lately? "I had a bit of a bad day yesterday," I said. "And today." Did I. "Sorry about that."

Mom hesitated before grasping my hand. "Not just recently," she said. Stopped again like she'd fought with herself about saying anything. I stared at her, mind rebelling against the suggestion I'd been anything but me prior to Sadie's comment while my heart made me accept Mom was right. My funk had been a long time growing. "Never mind," Mom said. "It's none of my business, and you're obviously feeling better." Her eyes twinkled before she covered her mouth with one hand, gaze widening. "I'm a horrible person."

I laughed and hugged her, awkward to do sitting down like that, but she hugged me back with the same level of enthusiasm I expected from a standing embrace. "Thanks, Mom," I said. "And you're not. Truth is, I've been feeling a bit lonely." There, I said it. "This wasn't how I expected my life to turn out." In fact, if anyone told me two years ago I'd be living in Reading again, running Grandmother Iris's B&B and adopted mother to a flatulent pug, I'd have laughed in their face before drowning the idea in a bottle of merlot.

Mom's patient empathy wasn't just for Olivia tonight. "It's been so hard for you," she said "coming back here like this. There are so few opportunities for you to meet anyone." She sipped her tea, deep red lipstick leaving a rim on her white mug. "I know you don't want to talk about your love life with your mother—"

"Non-existent love life," I said, meaning to be sarcastic but coming out rather pathetic.

"I'm just saying... any time you do need to talk, Fee. Honey, I'm here for you." Were those tears in her eyes? I hugged her again, quickly and emotionally myself, choking a bit on the rise of self-pity I quashed with my newly minted return to the real me.

"Thanks." I whispered that in her hair. "It means a lot. But I'm okay, I promise."

She leaned away, dabbing at her eyes with her

napkin. "It's been so wonderful having you home," she said, a little too brightly. "I don't want anything to drive you away again."

And then she was crying. I stood and embraced her fully, letting her weep into my shoulder, the stupid gold fluffy sweater, heart full and wishing there was something I could say. She had no idea how much I'd loved reconnecting with her, with Dad, after leaving Reading in a furious huff on the cusp of adulthood to go to college. How coming back here had meant the kind of fresh start I'd never expected to get with them.

Rather than talk about it, I just stood there and hugged her while she pulled herself together before she patted me on the arm, clear signal she was done. I sat again, Petunia humming her discontent that Mom was upset—or that we weren't feeding her, close enough—while Mom wiped the tears from her face, taking a good portion of her makeup with her.

"Love you, Mom," I said.

"Love you too, sweetie." She smiled through her tears, blinking fast, though her expression seemed genuinely happy.

The kitchen door swung inward, the interruption almost setting off my temper. Until I caught the sorrowful face of Emelia Cortez peeking in.

"I'm so sorry to intrude," she said, voice low and thick with weariness, "but I was hoping to trouble you for a cup of tea."

Mom was on her feet and all business, hustling right to Emelia and escorting her to the very stool she'd just vacated. "No trouble at all, my dear," she said, back into Lucy Fleming handling everything mode. "What flavor would you like?"

Daisy waved at me from the door and I went to join her while Mom dealt with our guest.

"I'm going to head home if you don't need me?" She glanced over my shoulder at my mother and Emelia chatting at the counter.

"You don't work here anymore, silly," I said. "Thank you so much, though." I never meant for that to cut her, so why did she flinch like she felt guilty?

"I shouldn't have dragged you to that séance tonight." Another hug, more emotion, though no tears this time. "It's my fault you were there, not yours."

Was she trying to comfort me? Trying to convince me I wasn't a death magnet? "I'm glad we were together," I said. "I'd hate for you to have been there alone."

She squeezed both of my hands in hers. "You're the best friend ever, Fee," she said. And fled.

Huh. Well, I had that going for me, I guess. Though I thought she fit that role a lot better than I did.

I turned back to find Mom seated next to Emelia, holding her hand, her eyes meeting mine with that kind of level comfort I loved about my mother. I joined them quietly, sipping my own tea, as Mom softly spoke.

"It's been six months then?" She nodded to me. "Since they lost their son."

I knew that already. And would have loved to ask questions, but it was terrible timing. Right? Mom didn't seem to think so. At least she didn't sound like she was curious, just supportive, where I was sure if I'd asked it would have sounded nosy.

Needed to take some Lucy lessons.

"That's right," Emelia said, staring into her cup. "It's been so hard, Lucy." First name basis already. Yup, Mom was in full mothering mode. "Not knowing what killed Manuel. Why he died. He was so young, so full of life. A gifted musician." She smiled then, through fresh tears. Had she been crying for half a year? I couldn't imagine. "Pianist. Brilliant. His playing would make you weep it was so beautiful."

"The police didn't have answers?" Mom didn't sound judging, just kind.

"None." Emelia's lips twisted, her lipstick long gone, beautiful face ravaged by grief. I'd thought she was maybe in her fifties, but the closer I looked, the more I realized her sorrow had aged her. "They found nothing. Said he'd died of a heart attack. At nineteen." She shook her head, black hair coming loose from the bun at the nape of her neck, a few strands falling over her shoulder. "And yet, there was nothing wrong with his heart."

"So you've been looking for answers," Mom said. "That's completely understandable."

Emelia smiled at her suddenly, nodding. "Yes, exactly. Amos doesn't believe, but I do. I do. I know my baby is trying to reach me." She leaned back, staring into the dark kitchen like she could see him in front of her. "I haven't been able to work, to even think. I've taken a hiatus from teaching because it wasn't fair to my students."

Mom perked. "What grade?"

Emelia shook her head. "I teach philosophy at Harvard."

My mother actually blushed, like her question had no merit all of a sudden. Why, just because the woman beside her taught at an Ivy League school? I'd never known Mom to judge herself for her talented days as principal at Reading High, and hoped she wasn't starting now. Though it did make me wonder about my mother's hopes and dreams, something I'd never considered before. She always seemed really happy teaching, running the school. Her baking was a recent love. Or did she settle like I'd almost done? I looked at her in a new, startled light as Mom went on.

"And your husband?" She recovered from her shift in mood, still soft and gentle.

It worked, I guess. "He's a partner at his law firm in Boston," she said. "He's done the opposite of me, thrown himself into work. Just when I need him the most." She sobbed, deep, wrenching sounds, though softly, apologetic like she expected to be judged. Didn't think much of Amos Cortez right about then.

Mom had bounced quickly back from her moment of embarrassment—what did she have to be ashamed of, anyway?—to speak up again, putting the woman first like she always did. "What led you to try paranormal means to find answers?"

Emelia barked a bit of a laugh, humorless and sharp edged. "What else was there? A friend suggested it, said the man she used helped her find her grandmother's missing pearls." Made me think of Iris for some reason, though I privately snorted over the idea. Like a faker of Sadie's ilk could help me uncover a pirate treasure that likely didn't exist. "The first psychic couldn't help, but I found Sadie online six weeks ago and she's been so precise. Knew things that she shouldn't have known." And yet, if she was using social media or more advanced tech to dig up info—tech I now suspected her grandson would have zero issues infiltrating if he designed that system she was using—it would be easy enough to lure a heartsick mother searching for answers. "I just knew I had to come here, to talk to her in person. To see my baby one more time." Her eyes flashed to mine then as she lurched toward me, grasping my fingers in hers, almost spilling my mug. She didn't seem to notice, gaze burning with need. "You were there, Fiona. You saw him. He tried to talk to me."

"I don't know what I saw," I said, refusing in that moment to make the cruel choice and tell her what I'd found, about the tech setup I knew Sadie used to trick her. Emelia didn't need to know. Yet. "But I do know the answer to your son's murder is out there, Emelia. And you have every right to find it." That much at least I was certain of.

She shivered slightly, let me go as if only realizing then she'd made contact. "You really think so?"

"I agree," a soft voice said. We all looked up, startled, to find Alice Moore watching us through her thick glasses, the faint light of the bulb over the stove making her hazel eyes invisible behind the shield of the lenses. "But not this way. What you saw tonight was a fraud, Dr. Cortez."

She had to go and do that, didn't she? Though I wasn't prepared for the reaction of the woman next to me. It was almost as if Emelia Cortez was seized by some kind of fit, her face turning deep red, eyes bulging when she spun on Alice, guttural protest turning to a thin shriek.

"HOW DARE YOU!" She lunged and I barely caught her before she hurtled herself at the startled young woman. The switch in emotion caught me so off guard I actually felt myself flinch. "You bitch, mind your own business!"

Whoa. Mom instantly acted while I clung to Emelia and did my best to keep the woman from attacking Alice who stood her trembling ground.

"Can we help you, dear?" Nothing like the whip crack of a former principal's practiced control to shut someone up. Fortunately, Mom's attitude seemed to diffuse Emelia's excessive temper, too, because she sagged slightly, whipping her head around to stare at my mother.

Alice actually gulped, sagged a little. "I'm sorry," she said. She looked up again and met my eyes. "I'm here for a room. Apparently I'm not to leave town just yet."

I went to her, abandoning Mom with the visibly steaming Emelia who now muttered incoherent Spanish with her face in a rictus of fury. Temper, temper. Rather than be an unwilling witness to a catfight in my kitchen, I opted to guide the young woman back out into the foyer with an attempt at a light-hearted joke. "Let me guess, the sheriff asked nicely."

Alice accepted the distraction, bright red cheeks returning to more normal pale slowly as she shrugged, her oversized blue sweater falling from one skinny shoulder, hand rising to absently tug it back into place. That same hand then pushed back her glasses as she answered. "Something like that."

Why was I not surprised?

CHAPTER TWELVE

EMELIA STORMED PAST US a moment later while Alice clutched her small bag of possessions, waiting for her key. The older woman didn't meet our eyes, but it was clear she was furious with the younger's attitude and intrusion on the lies she was telling herself. To each their own and while I disagreed with Alice's timing, I knew the truth would have to come out for the grieving mother eventually.

Mom joined us, a forced smile on her face. She'd borne the brunt of whatever blowup just happened to send Emelia Cortez stomping by, so I hardly blamed her for being irritated. Instead of letting her stew, I deflected Mom's anger at Alice with a soft question for my new guest.

"You're a debunker, aren't you?" There was no other reason for a stranger to be here in Reading at a séance with the kind of attitude and surety she'd just offered. Sadie practically said as much, commented on how Alice didn't need her to connect with the dead. From their brief and cryptic conversation tonight Alice had history with the now deceased, but how much history exactly? "Some kind of paranormal investigator?" I handed her credit card back while Alice nodded slowly.

"I have a blog," she shrugged. "I focus on uncovering frauds so the public know who not to trust." She tucked her card away, blinking behind her glasses. "It's not that I don't want the paranormal to exist." She sounded like it was the total opposite, emotion humming in her voice. "It's just that there are so many scammers out there taking advantage of people. I can't stand the idea that they are ripping grieving families off, good people. Like the Cortez's." She met Mom's eyes as I felt my mother relax somewhat beside me. "Sadie Hatch's scheme is more sophisticated than most." She sounded troubled by that, surprised. "While I do believe the dead can reach out to us, they don't do it through people like her." Okay, there was enough venom in her voice, well buried but present, I got the hint.

"You're sure it was all a show?" Mom bit her lower lip. "From what Emelia said, her son's ghost was far more real than the others Sadie tried to pretend were spirits." She glanced at me for approval and I nodded.

"I have to admit," I said, "she did a great job pulling that together." Suffered a shiver for the reminder.

Alice's hesitation told me she had some doubts or ideas she wasn't sharing. But when she spoke again, she sounded confident, if sad. "I know for a fact that woman was a fraud," she said. "Without a doubt. That the show she put on was just that, a hoax performance to take money from honest people and leave them with nothing but vague lies and half-truths she uncovered about them on the internet." We were on the same page there so I didn't argue. "Regardless of what Dr. Cortez or any of Sadie's clients might want to believe." She blinked a few times. "I didn't mean to hurt her like that," she said. "It's hard enough being in pain over the unexpected and unexplained loss of a loved one, but to have to face the fact the very thing you want is a fake... it's almost worse."

"You see a lot of this, then?" I grabbed her key, actually fascinated by the idea of being a paranormal detective. Could it be an option even Crew Turner wouldn't give me a hard time about? At least the people I'd be investigating would already be dead. Snort. Okay, not so funny, but yeah.

"Far too much." Alice paused, key in hand, bag over one shoulder. "Thank you. I can show myself up." She turned and headed for the stairs like she knew exactly where she was going, disappearing up the steps to the second floor without waiting for me to protest or guide her.

I let her find her way, mostly because my mind was spinning. She seemed so sure that Sadie's show was a fake, but I wasn't now. Not until I got a better look at that panel Sadie used to trigger the images. Yes, I was sure the static holographics she'd used were preset—I was looking right at the portrait of Iris she'd stolen right now, staring back at me from the bottom of the stairs. But Manuel's ghostly apparition, the way it moved, how it morphed itself, felt different, more advanced even than the cool tech I'd thought was above and beyond. Everything about that final encounter had been a step further than the rest.

Problem was, I had no excuse to go back to the house. And I was pretty sure if I tried, and was caught, Crew would finally arrest me, throw me in jail and toss the key as far from him as he could get.

Mom retreated to the kitchen again without a word, likely to clean up, while I closed off the computer for the night and locked the front door. Surely there would be no more late-night signups sent my way. If there were, the bell would warn me. Maybe the sheriff himself might show up...? Thinking about Crew made me twitch as I sighed and leaned my back against the door, staring down the hall at the kitchen.

I had to do something about him. Giving him a dating ultimatum felt like a really smarmy option. That meant letting go of the idea I might ever find out what being with him or what life with his handsome yumminess would be like. Thing was, I deserved to be happy. I knew that, logically. Waiting around for someone who might never make up his mind? Not a good recipe for living in bliss.

Okay then. Time to choose. Either ask him out myself and look desperate and lacking compassion for his loss—not going to happen—or start looking for someone else. I winced at that, though. The last guy I thought might be the one for me turned out to be a murdering thug and a drug addict who'd tried to kill me when I defended his real target, Willow Pink, from attack. So, could I ever trust my instincts when it came to men since the two guys I'd thought were right turned out to be a) a cheater and b) a murderer while the third was an unavailable grief stricken widow who alternated between despising me for poking my nose into his cases and being so kind I wanted to cry and hug him?

Sigh.

Not a good conversation to have with myself tonight. Because the new sparkly me wanted to head over to his house, throw the door open and ravage him until he forgot his wife in favor of hot blooded, redheaded me. Or, jump online and find a dating site or two to cruise, just to feel powerful while dodging the inevitable dick pics and requests to see me naked. Wait, I wanted to date again why?

Neither was a smart choice. Instead, I headed for the kitchen to round up my parents and send them both home.

Low voices emerged from behind the door and I half drew a breath to tell them to leave, when I pushed the swinging way open and found, not my mother and father, but Vivian French, her face tight with annoyance, facing off with Mom.

In my kitchen.

Oh no, she *didn't*.

She spotted me, grimaced like I had terrible timing before her face settled into cold calculation. "Nice snooping, Fiona," she snapped. "Way to piss off Crew."

"What are you doing here, Vivian?" I stomped to a halt beside Mom, wondering why she looked so pale, a faint smile plastered on her face that did nothing for the snap in her green eyes.

"She was just leaving," my mother said. Firmly.

Vivian tossed her head, spinning and storming out the kitchen door. Damn it, I'd never gotten around to fixing the gate by the driveway and I really needed to. Too many people knew how to slip through the back, apparently.

I turned to Mom, scowling, but she shook her head. "It's nothing." She chopped one hand through the air, the end of the conversation. Doubly so when Dad appeared at last, curiosity turning to concern as he realized we weren't happy.

"What?"

"Nothing." Mom repeated herself, heading for him with a scowl. "Where have you been?"

"Just talking with Amos," Dad said. His eyes lifted to mine, eyebrows climbing but I shook my head, crossing my arms over my chest.

"Fine," Mom said. "Let's go home." She stomped past Dad without another word to me while my heart hurt for the lost moment we'd shared earlier and vindictiveness took the place of that surge of mother/daughter awesome.

Whatever Vivian said to Mom, she was going to pay for upsetting her. Just as soon as I could get my hands on her.

CHAPTER THIRTEEN

OM AND DAD LEFT, him trailing after her, and I followed if only to relock the front door before returning to the kitchen to lock that one, too. Petunia and I made our way downstairs where I discarded the gold sweater firmly in the trash in my kitchen, dumping old coffee grounds and the leftover salad I'd failed to eat on top of it to make sure it was well and truly garbage.

Bad luck could take a flying leap.

I spent the next hour online, tucked under the covers with my laptop and my pug, pouring over the utterly fascinating blog of Alice Moore. Talk about a giant shocker. She wasn't just a paranormal debunking blogger, from what I could tell. She was *the* paranormal debunking blogger, covering everything from team reveals of fake footage in haunted locations to soothsayers and fortune tellers like Sadie Hatch. Though, as I perused the site, squeaking at the occasional video she shared that, while she'd uncovered as frauds, still made me jump, I realized she had a serious hate on for the old lady.

And, though Sadie had used that particular name in Reading, it was far from the only alias she used. That was, unless she had multiple sisters who looked just like her using totally different identities in a variety of states Alice seemed eager to uncover.

Huh. So what was it about Sadie—whoever she really was—that made Alice so very keen to tear her down and expose her in particular?

A quick leap into Reading's town directory told me the deceased was, in fact, Sadie Hatch. From here, in fact, daughter of William and Margaret Hatch. There wasn't much else in our local records, at least online. My own attempt to track her using the names Alice uncovered revealed a few hits in local newspapers around the country, petty fraud charges and some irate letters to the editor, as well as a fair number of warning posts in social media about her from those she'd ripped off along the way. But I didn't really learn much more than I'd already known and, eyes burning and 2AM fast approaching, I finally shut down my computer and my curiosity.

Six in the morning came much quicker than I would have liked, but I stumbled out of bed anyway, yawning my way through my first cup of coffee, a hot shower, before padding upstairs with Petunia to let her out. She dragged her own butt in weariness, not wanting to get out of bed, and I finally had to carry her up the stairs and scoot her outside to do her business.

None of my guests had risen yet, at least from what I could tell, so I went about my early routine, checking emails, prepping breakfast, waiting for Mom to arrive at seven. Sunlight streamed into the kitchen, warming the tiles though the nights were cooler and summer long over. I fell into the puttering familiarity of my life with ease, though when I found myself humming over a filling bucket of sudsy water, mop waiting beside me to do its duty on the floor, I paused.

Happiness wasn't tied to cleaning floors. And yet, I was content, wasn't I? Despite the feelings I'd been having, the loneliness I now knew fed my funk and gloom, it was nice to know that being here, running

Petunia's, actually did feed my soul. The rest of it, well, that was up to me. But it was comforting to accept I loved it here, I really, honestly did. No booby prize, not a second best choice. I was exactly where I wanted to be and doing what I loved.

A delightful revelation at 6:30 in the morning.

I was humming when I scrubbed, then, making my way from the back door to the exit, Petunia's breakfast long devoured as she backed out of my way with the long familiar grunting of habit. I closed the door softly on the damp floor, knowing it would be dry by the time Mom arrived, leaving the bucket and mop where they were as I turned to the front desk to check my messages.

No matter my own personal ideas about Olivia and her mayorship, the choices she'd made, she had kept my place full since day one, with only the odd break to give me a much needed rest. Today's long line of requests was no exception, the benefits of a driven leader showing in the long lineup on my cancellation list. It really was too bad I didn't have more space.

Mom's arrival broke me out of my train of thought. I had all I needed, right here in Petunia's. The only official game in town aside from the Lodge,

I was busy enough as it was. Money didn't matter, I had more than enough. If I was a bigger operation, I'd have less time.

For what, exactly? I paused at that thought as I checked over the third floor, despite the fact no one stayed there in the last two days. Habit, really. Well, for... my personal life. I clenched my jaw against my gut reaction to the lack of one and closed the door to the room I peeked into, cheery sunlight washing over the bed and leaving the faintest trail of dust motes in the air. Right. The quiet of my home was a great place to spend much-needed time to think, though sometimes I wondered if I did too much thinking for my own good.

As for today, it seemed fortuitous and a great time to address my loneliness. Make inroads on a real, honest to goodness social life.

I trotted downstairs, knowing there was no time like the present. Instead of researching last night I should have been signing up for dating sites, right? Well, I could do that right now, while Mom made up breakfast and things were quiet enough I could actually consider dating.

Might even be fun.

I was almost to the foyer, considering my

options, when the front door opened and Jared Wilkins walked through. He looked up as I slowed, waving to him as he waved back, a faint frown on his face fading as he smiled. While he was Pete's son, he favored his attractive mother. And though stress had increased the line between his eyes, he was still young and handsome enough I had to mentally smack myself at the thought that raced through my head.

Blamed it on my present plan to find a partner. Because Jared was far too young for me, not to mention the fact he was taken.

"Hey, Fee," he said, deep voice soft. I joined him, grinned a little shakily.

"Hi, Jared. What's up?" Up close he looked tired, and I wondered how much his father's misdeeds weighed on him. Not my business, but I liked him, and his girlfriend, Alicia.

"I hoped we could talk about something." He hesitated. "I was going to call, but I thought seeing you in person might be the better way to go."

Uh-oh. Why did that make me nervous? He shifted his feet, swallowed. Seemed anxious himself all of a sudden. Was there something wrong? About Petunia's? His father had a signed deed that my grandmother agreed to only to catch Pete in the act of stealing properties from the aged at the nursing home his sister ran. But Jared told me long ago he'd negated that paperwork. Had something gone wrong?

My heart leaped into my throat at the thought of losing this place, and I'm sure I paled because Jared's odd behavior turned to concern as he reached out and caught my arm in one hand.

"It's nothing bad, I swear," he said. "Sorry, I shouldn't have scared you. Especially after the night you had."

Phew. I exhaled, feeling the world expand again from the tightness in my chest and the fear thudding my pulse. I forced a smile, relaxing a little, though now I was worried about him, despite his assurance.

He opened his mouth to speak the second my cell phone rang. And laughed, gesturing for me to answer my buzzing butt. I did, grinning now, barely hitting the answer button when Aundrea's panicked voice reached me.

"Fee!" She shouted so loud I know Jared heard her when I jerked the phone back from my ear. "You have to come, now!"

"Aundrea?" I frowned at her son who shook his head in confusion. "What's going on?"

"That bastard of a sheriff just arrested Pamela," she said, her panic clear in her voice. "I need your help!"

CHAPTER FOURTEEN

E WHAT? "I'LL BE right there." I hung up, eyebrows raised at Jaren who shrugged.

"No clue," he said. "I'll go get Alicia and meet you at the sheriff's office."

He left before he could tell me what he wanted, while my mind asked me why his mother called me and not him. There'd be time later for both questions to be answered, once I figured out why Crew would think Pamela murdered Sadie Hatch. Dad appeared as Jared left, frowning when I spun on him, raising my phone like evidence.

"Could use some backup," I said. "Feel like pissing off the sheriff?"

Dad's white teeth flashed. "After you, pumpkin."
Why did I laugh at the sound of evil glee in his voice?

He drove, parking right out front in a spot reserved for one of the cruisers. I didn't comment, though I was pretty sure Robert would eat himself alive knowing Dad took his spot. I glanced over my shoulder as my cousin picked the perfect time to pull up, speak of the devil, waving at his hateful face as he glared at the car in his place before sullenly driving further down the street.

Dad never said anything negative to me about his nephew, his sister's only son, even when I was young and bitter about Robert's attitude toward me. While I knew he would never take that jerk's side against me, my father's silence over Robert's attempt to bully me and subsequent stint at the academy that ended with him working under Dad in Reading, had left me with a bad taste in my mouth. One I never really acknowledged fully until that moment. The wink Dad tossed me, followed by an eye roll of epic proportions, spoke more volumes than an actual explanation of his opinion could have. Dad rose to even further heights in my estimation with that gesture before opening the door so I could enter. How gentlemanly of him. And what a beautiful, bright and sunshiny day it was all of a sudden.

We marched into confusion and a lot of shouting—mostly Aundrea—while Crew did his best to shut her down. She spun the moment we appeared, gesturing for us to join them, still talking at full volume. So recently buoyed by Dad's support in the Robert department, I went to her despite having no idea if I could actually help or not.

"When my lawyer gets here you can be absolutely certain I'll be suing this town, this department and you personally, Crew Turner, for this travesty of justice." She shook so hard her perfectly styled hair was in disarray, face red with emotion. Pamela stood next to her, trying to soothe her with a soft hand on her arm, whispering to her, but Aundrea wasn't listening. Not to her partner and not to the rapidly devolving temper now showing on Crew's handsome face, made worse when he glanced our way.

"Aundrea." Dad's deep, steady voice silenced her like nothing else had been able to.

"John." Her voice trembled now, her distress turning from anger to fear. "This is preposterous."

Dad nodded to her, then to Crew. "I take it there's evidence you're considering against Pamela?"

Crew exhaled heavily, jaw so tight I worried he

might crack a molar. But he pulled himself under control, hands on his hips, head lowering like a bull ready to charge.

"I have questions," he stressed, "for a witness," he glared at Aundrea before going on, "in an ongoing investigation I still don't know is an actual crime or not." That done, he straightened. "No one has been arrested. Yet."

The door banged open, Olivia choosing the perfect moment to enter, her face set, a full head of steam built up. Crew exhaled explosively and tossed his hands, a muttered, "I give up," all he got out before she was in his face.

"What is the meaning of this?" She spun toward Aundrea, patted her arm. "Honestly, Sheriff Turner, your conduct—"

"I REPEAT." He roared it that time, utter silence falling as shocked faces stared at him. "NO ONE. IS UNDER. ARREST." A full ten seconds of silence followed while he met every set of eyes individually, including Dad's and mine. "Now," he said at a much more reasonable tone, as if the outburst had given him the release he needed to carry on, "if you'll all just let me do my damned job, I'd like to talk to Pamela about last night." He glared at Aundrea, at

Olivia. "Alone."

"My lawyer—" Aundrea wasn't quitting.

"Pam," Crew spun on the newspaper woman. "Do you need a lawyer?"

"I don't know," she said, quiet and confident. "Do I need one, Crew?"

He shrugged. "Did you kill anyone last night?"

She snorted a laugh. "Let's get this over with."

Crew turned and marched away, past the swinging wooden gate that was the half-wall barrier between the reception area and the bullpen. With a quick hug and smile for Aundrea, Pamela followed and, without pausing or a hint of hesitation, Dad went with her.

I'll give it to Crew. He didn't lose his mind, or his temper. He stopped as Pamela entered his office, one hand rising to stop my father from going after her.

Neither of them spoke, but the standoff lasted long enough I knew Dad wasn't going to let it go. Except, about five seconds in, he nodded, backed off. And watched with an unreadable expression as Crew closed the door firmly behind him.

Jared and Alicia's breathless arrival stirred things up again, but the heated moment of explosion was diffused, over with. Olivia turned, looking equally lost and flustered, as if she'd failed somehow. Her eyes locked on mine before she could sort herself out.

"I expected you in my office this morning." She huffed that out. "I don't like being left waiting." She glanced at Jared who shook his head just enough I knew they were in on whatever it was she wanted to talk about.

"And I don't like being pushed around," I shot back. "Maybe if you ask next time."

I expected her to argue, to give me lip. Instead, she left in a huff, Aundrea sinking into her son's arms while Alicia comforted her, eyes meeting mine with genuine concern. Not the right time to grill Jared about what the hell was going on, apparently, though I was tempted.

Robert stomped inside, taking all of us in with one look before deciding throwing his weight around was a good idea. Not.

"Unless you have business with the sheriff," he said in that tone of voice that I'm sure he thought made him sound special—I bet he practiced it in front of a mirror while watching cop shows, the loser—"you're to vacate the premises. Immediately."

"You kicking me out, young man?" Dad's voice,

on the other hand, was quiet. So very quiet. How satisfying to see Jill, firmly ensconced now at the gate to keep us out, grin suddenly before smothering her humor with a blank expression and Robert blanch.

While Toby Miller, the office receptionist and a huge fan of my father's, looked up at Dad with the kind of adoration that made me wonder if she even considered Crew her sheriff.

Robert fishlipped a bit before Jared sighed, leading his mother out.

"We'll be back," he said over his shoulder. "With our lawyer."

Hopefully it wouldn't come to that. Surely Pamela of all people, being a reporter, wouldn't willingly talk if she had anything to hide. Not without representation. As for Crew, I trusted he had his heart in the right place, wasn't out to get anyone. He'd come out and said he didn't have evidence Sadie's death was foul play. Talking to Pamela was merely a formality, then, one Aundrea blew way out of proportion for some reason. Panic wasn't necessary. So I found myself unwinding a bit, too, while Dad slipped past Jill with a nod before smiling at Toby who rose in a rush to hug him.

"Nice to see you," he said. "How's Henry?" She

straightened her fleece vest with the sheriff's department logo—her favorite accessory—and beamed up at Dad, a full foot shorter than him.

I left them to talk, drifting over to Jill while Robert brushed past her and stomped to his desk where he noisily started sorting paperwork that obviously had no need of such attention.

"Fun times," I said.

"You're telling me." She eye rolled. "He's such a princess." Was she talking about Robert or Crew? From the sidelong look of suffering she shared with me, my cousin was her target. For the moment, anyway.

I choked out a snort. "I meant the case."

She grinned back. "Yeah. Right. Me too."

I glanced at Crew's door, keeping my voice down as I spoke. "Does he know Sadie had aliases?"

She started briefly, also casting her eyes toward his office. "How did you find out?"

I filled her in on Alice's blog. Jill nodded quickly, though we both caught Robert watching with hateful eyes.

"Thanks," Jill said. "I'll check it out."

"So you didn't know?"

"Just that she has history with Pamela." Jill

flinched then, looked away. "Robert's on background checks." She stopped herself again. "I can't talk about it, Fee." She cleared her throat, caught my eyes again, hers widening just slightly. While Robert leaned closer, eavesdropping, the ass. Why, so he could rat her out? Jerk.

She had orders to keep her mouth shut. Fair enough. And not fair of me to ask when her job was at stake. I nodded, smiled so she knew I understood while internally yelling at Crew for trusting something as important as background checks to the likes of Robert Carlisle.

"Come have coffee with me and Daisy on the weekend," I said. "It would be nice to hang out."

Jill flashed me another smile. "Will do."

I turned back to Dad, subtly flipping Robert my middle finger, knowing he saw and grinning like an idiot about it. Juvenile, maybe, but so satisfying.

Dad grabbed my arm before I could come to a complete halt, a quick kiss for Toby's cheek as he did, shoving me ahead of him while we made our exit without another word. He was chortling to himself.

Never a good sign. "What did you do?"

He winked at me. "Let's go to Petunia's," he said, "and I'll show you."

CHAPTER FIFTEEN

I HUNCHED OVER MY laptop, now resting on the kitchen counter, and sat next to Dad as his thick fingers tapped with far more agility than I gave him credit for while his lowered voice filled me in. Not that Mom wasn't well aware we were up to shenanigans—her word—but I had the feeling he was having far too much fun and if he raised his voice he'd be shouting.

Who was this man and where did he put my normally stoic, quiet and reserved father? Then again, as the screen lit up with the Reading Sheriff's Department website and I gulped over the FBI or worse flagging my IP address for unauthorized access to a police data base, Dad tapped in a password that took us to a further screen while he wriggled on his chair in utter delight.

"What are we doing?" Okay, so if the FBI—yes, I was overthinking this into worst possible scenario—was going to come to my door and ask me questions, I should at least know what the hell I'd be interrogated about. My nervousness went away when Dad started cruising the site like he owned it. Well, he had been sheriff for a long time, so it wasn't like the inner workings of his former department were a mystery to him. Me, on the other hand? I watched in fascination as he brought up Sadie Hatch and her profile.

"You stole the password from Toby, didn't you?" I chided him gently while his slight flash of guilt was washed away with a wink.

"She doesn't know and Crew doesn't have to," he said. "She always keeps it under her blotter. I just moved it when I hugged her."

Of course he did. "You're a horrible, horrible person."

Dad laughed. Like a kid caught with his hand in the cookie jar and most of the contents already in his stomach. He was actually having fun. That made me wonder just what he gave up when he retired.

"Okay," he said. "Here we go. Sadie Louise Hatch, born here in Reading." I knew that, didn't comment. "Goes by a list of aliases." He ran his finger down the screen, frowning. "Crew dug up a fair amount so far." Grudging scrap of respect there for Robert, but I refused to tell Dad it was his nephew behind the info. He was a smarmy piece of work, but maybe my cousin did know what he was doing. Maybe. "Petty theft, fraud charges, a few misdemeanor public nuisance things. Nothing big, Fee. Mostly under the radar."

"Nothing big? No blackmail or straight up theft?" I guess it would be hard to prove she stole from people if they willingly hired her.

He shook his head. "She might have a list a mile long, but her worst offense is faking her identity." Dad tapped his fingers on the counter. "It's a felony offense, could lead to jail time, but looks like no one ever caught her while she was in their jurisdiction. And since she was using her real name here, Crew's not on the hook for missing it."

"So what does Pamela have to do with this?" I didn't bother telling Dad I already knew what the sheriff did, about Sadie's aliases. Or that it had seemed like Pamela and Sadie had a past. In fact, the more I thought about it, the more I wondered what Pamela had against the dead woman and if the grandmother image the fake psychic "raised" had anything to do with it. I went over her reaction during the séance and couldn't help but make that connection.

Dad hummed softly while he dug deeper, Mom finally interrupting. She leaned over his shoulder, expression deepening into a frown, not her normal state of face. In fact, she'd been pretty quiet since last night, after her encounter with Vivian. I'd brushed off Mom's silence this morning because I'd been busy. But come to think of it, she hadn't been herself. And it showed when she spoke, bitterness in her tone unbecoming Lucy Fleming.

"This is Crew's job, John." I'd never heard her chastise him, especially with anything resembling resentment. Mom had handled Dad's career choice and long hours with nothing but solid support and good natured patience. "Considering there's no evidence of actual wrong doing at this point, maybe you should leave him to it?"

Dad didn't comment, ah-haing a moment later like he didn't even hear her. "Looks like Pamela might have had an altercation with her ten years ago," he said. No longer in the department's files, but doing what I'd done, he cruised the internet for clues.

Mom tsked in frustration. I reached out to take her hand but she turned her back on us and returned to the dishwasher she was loading. I was getting up to help her, wincing I'd left the job to her despite knowing she'd tell me she was fine, when Dad spoke again.

"Ended in an assault charge on Pamela's end."

Interesting, my favorite word these days. I sank back to my stool, elbows on the counter, frowning at the news report he'd uncovered. "She was definitely agitated at the séance," I said. "Like they'd met. But I had no idea." If Pamela assaulted the old woman previously, why would Sadie welcome her that night? Did she not recognize her? Or not care one way or another?

Dad gnawed his bottom lip, frowning at the screen like it should be giving him more than it had so far. "I don't know."

"And," I said, "after ten years—not to mention a whole year of Sadie being back here—why would Pamela try to kill her now if she was going to act at all?"

"If you two will excuse me," Mom interrupted,

voice sharp, "I need the counter to start tea."

Right, afternoon tea. Kind of a staple around here now. Though it was hours off, I took the hint and backed off, but Dad didn't seem to have heard her. Mom prodded him firmly with a spatula and he finally rose, taking the laptop with him out of the kitchen and our sight.

She glared after him, a stunning redhead in an apron and wielding a spatula like a weapon as if she wanted to smack him with it. For the briefest moment I watched resentment cross her face once again, that unfamiliar strain that appeared since last night making a deeper impression and my breath caught.

"Mom?"

She turned toward me then, flare of whatever she was fighting with gone, though any good humor she might be able to muster vanished with it.

"I would think the last thing you'd want would be to interfere with another murder investigation." Um, what? Mom seemed to flinch internally before she shook her head. "Out, Fee," she said then, a bit of regret in her tone, softening but not with her usual kindness, just enough to take the edge from her hasty words. "I just need to work."

I left dutifully, wanting to ask her if she was okay but unable to muster the words. Something happened last night, something Vivian would pay for. Mom was a grown woman, though, and despite her unusual reaction, I decided work was exactly what I needed to do too. While it hurt, Mom was absolutely right. I had a business to run, dating sites to sign up for. I might have witnessed a death that may or may not have been murder, but I sure as hell didn't need to investigate it to find out which.

Did I?

I spent the next hour scrubbing the bathrooms of the Carriage House in preparation for new guests due to arrive the next day, then tackling the final flower bed next to the door. I jerked dead, brown plants from the soil, dumping them with vigor into the wheel barrow, taking out my waffling emotions that ranged from anger at Mom for being mean and Crew for not making up his damned mind and myself for letting any of it get to me.

By the time I had the bed all cleaned and put to bed for the winter, I was tired, dirty and relaxed. Something about digging around in the ground had a soothing effect on me. I straightened, wiping my forehead with the back of my gardening glove, sighing into the fading warmth of late morning, only then noticing Petunia had meandered her way out to join me. She lay on her side in the sun, catching the rays in a sheltered spot, snorting softly in her sleep.

I grabbed the handles of the wheelbarrow, hoisting it and starting my trundling way back to the main house and the compost heap I'd been cultivating behind a row of bushes to hide it from the guests. It was sheltered enough no one knew it was there, but got great light and, as I dumped my latest deposit, was aging nicely while the vegetation I added to it turned slowly to the most amazing potting soil ever.

Job done, mind on lunch, I was about to head back to the house when I heard voices. Alice's was easy enough to identify, but it took me a moment to realize the male one was Oliver.

"—her death had nothing to do with me." He sounded furious. "I can't believe you asked me to come here to talk about this. You could have come to me at the shop."

"That deputy has been watching your store," Alice said. Who, Robert? "He gives me the creeps." Yup, Robert. "I was just asking a question, Oliver."

"She's kept her distance since she came back," he

grumbled. "I barely saw her. I had no reason—"

"After what happened between you," Alice said, "I thought I'd make sure. That's all. You know the sheriff will be asking, too."

Oliver grunted. "It was a long time ago." Silence a moment, and then, "Considering your past with her, I'd think you'd want to mind your own business, young lady."

Well now. How interesting. And I know I would have learned more if it hadn't been for the untimely waking and aroused interest of my pug. Petunia, snorting free of her sleep across the garden, jerked awake, barking her delight at visitors, waddling over to greet them before hurrying past them and right to me.

Um, oops. Now who was eavesdropping?

Both Alice and Oliver seemed shocked to find me there and, before I could say a word, they turned and left, Alice going into the house, Oliver circling the path toward the side gate.

That was it. I was fixing that thing today, end of story.

CHAPTER SIXTEEN

GRUMBLING TO MYSELF—I'D decided to stay out of it, so why was the Universe conspiring to keep me in it?—I headed for the kitchen. Mom was quiet, almost silent, grunting the occasional noncommittal response to my attempt at false cheer so I gave up, leaving her to putter around the kitchen, Petunia fed and napping.

I cleaned up quickly, a text coming through as I wiped my hands, dropping my kitchen towel in the sink, the quiet of my apartment making the following feel like I was sneaking around.

Crew let her go. I'm still calling my lawyer. Only Aundrea would text in full sentences. *Thanks for earlier. I'll keep you posted.* Long pause and then another ding. *She's innocent.*

I know, I sent back. *All good.*

I stared into the sunbeam shining through my window and sighed. I was not going to go talk to Pamela about Sadie. I was not going to leave this bed and breakfast and poke my nose in any more. Robert's jabs about me being nosy lingered, because I knew he was right. I *was* a busybody, had been my whole life. Coming home to Reading hadn't changed that. Made me wonder how I'd missed my ex's cheating for so long. Unless I wanted to miss it.

That was a sadly chilling and depressing thought that only made matters worse. Convinced me once and for all I wasn't going to pass the doors of this place ever again, that leaving the poking and prodding up to Crew and his staff, as much as it felt like I'd failed for some weird reason, was my only option from now on.

I was done being that girl who didn't mind her own damned business.

Done.

Yeah. Right.

Ten minutes later I stood outside Aundrea's, waiting for the chime of the bell to go quiet, guilty over my total lack of willpower but itching inside with a rash only answers could scratch. Aundrea jerked the door wide, tears on her cheeks, her face pale and blotchy from distress and suddenly I was glad I ignored my wiser, more logical mind so I could be there for her.

"Pamela's not here," she said. "I don't know where she went. But she came home for five minutes, got a file out of her office and left."

I followed her inside, stood there in her huge front entry and waited for her to pull herself together before asking the obvious.

"Aundrea, what does Pamela have against Sadie?" The assault from ten years ago had to have a cause, and who better to ask than the woman she loved?

Apparently she was as in the dark as I was. "I have no idea." Aundrea tossed her hands before dabbing at her tears with a crumpled tissue. "Pam left when I married Pete, was gone for a long time. She was so angry, we both were. I never thought I'd see her again. I was furious at her for abandoning me, but it wasn't her fault, Fee." More information than she had to share, but I appreciated how much hurt she still carried around and let her talk, wondering how a relationship could survive such damage and shaking that out of my consciousness before it could take root. "She only came back a few years before you did." I didn't know that, but it made sense. The assault charge happened in a small town outside St. Louis, not Reading. "We made up shortly after her return. I made sure of that." A sharp nod, a sniff as she settled, brow furrowed. "But no matter how much I asked, she won't tell me much about her time away from me. Apart from the fact that she worked as a reporter."

Hardly a shocker. She was our town's only newspaperwoman and gained her skills somewhere. "No guesses, nothing at all?"

Aundrea's fear and anxiety were so real I shivered when she grasped my wrist in one shaking hand, her eyes huge. "All I know is something horrible happened," she said. "Fee, I know what I said in the sheriff's office, but…"

But.

"Do you think Pamela killed Sadie?" No way. Couldn't be.

Aundrea sagged. "She carries so much anger inside her." She whispered that like it was a betrayal. "I hardly blame her. It's my fault." I wanted to ask an uncomfortable question, but before I could find a way to voice it, Aundrea shook her head, nails digging into my arm. "She doesn't take it out on me," she said. "I almost wish she would. I deserve it." Her family had a lot to answer for. The Pattersons had not just separated two women who loved each other for no good reason aside from their own stupid pride, but they'd done a great deal of damage in the process. The kind of wounds that lingered and drove blades through hearts. "It was her idea to go that night," Aundrea finally blurted after a shaking moment of silence. "And she acted funny, Fee. Like she had something to hide from me. Until that woman was dead. And then... she seemed relieved."

Not good. But not proof of any wrongdoing, either.

I left then, promising if I found Pamela I'd make her call home, doing my best not to pry further into her private life. Maybe I should have, but I wasn't anyone's shrink and in no kind of position to offer comfort. With the terrible luck I was now known for, I'd make things worse.

Bad enough Aundrea's husband died in my koi pond. No way was I going to be the cause of conflict between her and Pamela. I might be a nosy busybody, but I drew the line at hurting my friends.

Didn't keep me from hunting for answers of another kind. My next obvious port of call, the Reading Reader Gazette office, was closed, not a sign Pamela had been there. Looked like she'd given her office staff the day off, too, though they were part timers, so for all I knew I was after hours anyway. I stared in frustration at the locked door, knowing going home was the best choice right now. I had my own stuff to deal with, my business to run. This was ridiculous. But, as I turned to march back to Petunia's and bury my curiosity in a pile of laundry, I instead came to a squeaking halt just before I ran right into the quivering, startled form of Denver Hatch.

CHAPTER SEVENTEEN

W E BOTH STOPPED, STARTLED, but he looked far more nervous than he should have considering he'd known I was there. I reached out on impulse, tried to grab his hand, to say something to comfort him for the loss of his grandmother—fraud or not, she was his family—when he spoke. Well, blurted. "Where is she?" Took me a second to make the connection and when I did I almost facepalmed. Of course he was here for the same reason as me, but why? Like Pamela was meant to meet him here, maybe? He bent sideways to look past me into the dark office, face twisting in anxiety.

"I don't know." I was rather proud of that calm,

level tone I'd adapted from a mix of Dad at his most quiet and Mom's practiced control over crazy teenagers for over thirty years. "Can I help you with something, Denver?" Right, because a random stranger was exactly who he'd hoped to encounter here.

He shook his head, pulling his hand away, using it to grasp his opposite forearm, the air of utter dejection about him making me worry for his state of mind.

"I just wanted to apologize," he whispered.

"For what?" Wow, Fee, way to act all grown up and be kind and not blurty yourself. Wicked.

Denver's eyes caught mine, misery embedded deep. "For my grandmother," he said. "How things went down. Pamela..." he shook his head then, turned away before I could stop him, and ran. Jerking, out of control, gone while I tsked in frustration over losing him like that.

What had Sadie done to Pamela that warranted the kind of reaction he was having? Or was there more to Denver's clear decline than he was saying? If he knew about Sadie's misdeeds, if he found he couldn't live with her fraud and hurting people any longer... could he have killed his own grandmother?

I shook myself briefly. Yet again I had to remind myself there was no proof she'd been murdered, remember? Nothing that I knew of, anyway. From what Dr. Aberstock said, while a huge coincidence, it could have been a heart attack at the most inopportune of moments. A thought passed through my mind, brief and rife with conspiracy theories. Could she have faked her own death in order to avoid some kind of persecution? But no, I was there when she died, when the doctor checked her over. Unless she had some kind of magic wand or was an alien—I had to get out more—she wasn't coming back from the dead.

Unless ghosts *were* real, then all bets were off.

With nothing else to do besides argue with myself about being a good girl and avoiding the rest of the case like the plague, I went home. For a brief moment I considered stopping at the bakery, to have a not-so-friendly chat with Vivian about staying away from my mother. Instead, not in the mood to end a fight she started by daring to say a word to Mom, I instead strode past, the scent of yeasty bread in the air, hating that it made my stomach growl.

She could keep her freshly baked goods. I hoped she choked on them.

Lunch was already underway, our expanded dining hours now covering tea in the afternoon and a small selection of soups and sandwiches Mom was experimenting with. I winced when I hurried inside, not because I was late. She was more than capable of handling the dozen or so locals who came to delight in her offerings. In fact, I knew how much she loved to manage the entire process herself, that the adoration of her regulars gave her a real perk. No, it wasn't Mom I was worried about.

It was Dad. And the sight of him facing off with Malcolm Murray in the foyer. Whoops. Forgot to mention to my father the Irish bar owner liked to frequent Petunia's on occasion. Mind you, if I knew why specifically Dad didn't want Malcolm around—aside from the fact the man was a criminal—maybe I'd be behind keeping the Irishman from coming over. But he'd never been anything but straight up with me, implying, as a matter of fact, he and Dad had a history neither of them were willing to share.

So seeing them arguing quietly, voices so low I couldn't make out details though their body language gave away the height of tension between them, triggered my curiosity all over again.

Before I could approach them and ask them to

finally just spill already, Malcolm turned from Dad and stormed out, past me as if he didn't even see me, a thundercloud of anger in his eyes. I let him go, staring at Dad, waiting for him to tell me what was going on.

Instead, he took his temper out on me. Naturally. "How long has he been coming here?"

I shrugged, kept it casual, refusing to let my own anger out. Because I was mad, make no mistake. Whatever this secret was, it had something to do with me, I was positive of it. While Dad might have thought he was protecting me or some other misguided notion my father was an expert at cultivating, I had the right to know what was going on.

"He's a resident of Reading. And since he's never been charged with anything," I stressed that truth, guessing to be honest, but Dad's flinch told me I was right, "and he continues to be pleasant and doesn't cause trouble, he's welcome here."

Dad shook his head. I thought Malcolm's scowl was dark and threatening. My father looked positively enraged, cheeks red, cords in his neck standing out. "Damn it, Fee," he snapped, "this isn't a joke."

"I wasn't joking." I approached him slowly, like a

matador facing off with a decidedly testy bull, but determined to get him to talk to me at last. "Dad, what is this about? What aren't you telling me?"

He shook off the question, looking away, staring at the door as if he could shatter it with his will alone. "I'll talk to Crew. Time to run that garbage out of town once and for all."

Another encounter ending in the guy I was trying to converse with taking off on me. Apparently that was how my day was going to go. I glared after Dad as he stomped out, a mix of fear and frustration almost pushing me to follow him. But he was in no shape to answer me, and though I was now more determined than ever to find out what was going on, I let him leave without comment, instead turning and heading for the kitchen.

I didn't quite make it, pausing while Amos exited the dining room, a tray with two bowls of soup, a small pile of sandwiches and two cups of coffee level in his hands. I reached out to take it but he shook his head with a faint smile, crinkling the corners of his dark eyes.

"You've been more than kind, as has your charming mother." He looked past me toward the stairs before meeting my gaze again. "Emelia just wasn't up to coming down for lunch."

"I'm happy to help," I said. "Let me know if you need anything." My empathy for them both hit harder than I expected as I watched his face crumple slightly before he nodded, trying another smile.

"Thank you," he said. "It's been… difficult."

"Having someone manipulate you and your wife couldn't have been easy either," I said. Yikes, did I really just start that conversation? Maybe he really did believe in Sadie.

But Amos just shrugged. "I knew the woman was a fraud," he said. "Emelia has been inconsolable. And it's only money, Miss Fleming. I have lots of that."

My heart broke a little, tears stinging the corners of my eyes. "Has there been any movement on your son's case?"

Amos's eyes tightened, a flare of anger deep inside them. Understandable, though he seemed to fight it before he spoke. "None," he said. "I handled enough criminal cases of my own when I was an assistant district attorney to know what the detectives told us was true. If it was foul play and Manuel was murdered, the likelihood of catching the killer diminishes exponentially after forty-eight hours." I had to agree, at least from what Dad had told me and from my own research into crime. Hey, I had the right to at least study what I found so interesting even if I wasn't going to actively pursue it as a career. Yup, sure, Fee, not creepy or anything. Carry on, then. "But the medical examiner still isn't convinced it was murder, despite what Emelia believes. As far as he could tell, Manuel died of a heart attack." The tray shook just slightly in his hands, some kind of reaction to his own admission, perhaps. "I know it's a horrible thing to say, but I'm in line for a nomination to the bench." A judge, wow. "It might be selfish, but if Manuel did die of natural causes, I'd like this chapter closed." He flinched, guilt clear. "I wish she would just let him go."

Well, I could hardly blame him for that, or the way his face twisted into a grimace, dark gaze far away. "Hopefully some kind of resolution will come about," I said, knowing that was a weak attempt at comfort but he seemed to accept it at face value, nodding to me with a new, real smile.

"I'm sure it will all work out somehow," he said. "Emelia's grief, while understandable, can't last forever." He seemed to realize what he'd just said. "And my own, of course."

She'd mentioned he'd thrown himself into work after the boy died. Everyone dealt differently and it wasn't up to me to be Amos's conscience.

"If you'll excuse me." He stammered, flustered. "I should go upstairs before this gets cold."

CHAPTER EIGHTEEN

I WATCHED HIM GO, heart hurting, wishing I could help. Maybe I could peek at the case, see if there was anything the detectives missed—

And sighed, turned back to the kitchen and forced myself to keep going. Because sure, Fee, untrained you with a terrible track record for getting into trouble that had nothing to do with you is going to crack an investigation that was likely natural causes because you might see something the pros missed.

I really had to get my priorities sorted out.

Mom hustled, her normally happy expression missing, though when I hurried to try to help her she scowled at me before jabbing her stirring spoon at Petunia. The pug huddled in the corner, looking pathetic and sad, cringing under my mother's furious gaze.

"Take that dog out of my kitchen!"

Um, wow. "Mom, are you ok—"

"Now, Fiona!"

Okie dokie, then.

I scooted the pug outside, noting her drooping tail, her lack of bubbliness that was my dog's normal and wondered what happened between her and my normally kindhearted and tolerant mother to end in this kind of a downcast state. Petunia paused on the walk, looking up at me with the saddest expression. I dropped to a crouch and hugged her, scratching her ears, whispering to her.

"It's not your fault, pug," I said. "She's just in a crappy mood. It's okay. You're a good girl, aren't you, Petunia?"

By the time I leaned away she was grinning at me, tail coiled over her butt, wriggling a bit in her returned happiness. What I wouldn't give for that kind of happy-go-lucky resilience. I kissed her wrinkled forehead and stood, following her as she trundled off through the garden.

Leaving me to worry about not only my father, but my mother, too. Lovely.

I didn't have much time to process my concerns for my parents and their present states of separate angst, not when I had my own to deal with. I was lost in thoughts not really worthy of me when my pug yipped a happy greeting, abandoning me for greener pastures. Petunia had found a friend by the rose bushes, feet up on the bench where Alice sat with her legs folded in lotus. She'd clearly been meditating and my pug interrupted. I rushed over to drag the dog away, but Alice was smiling kindly so I slowed my pace, offering a quick apology.

"I was almost done," Alice said. "Besides, there's nothing more soothing to the heart and mind than the emotional openness of an animal."

Pretty deep, but I wasn't going to argue. There were enough nights I'd found myself hugging Petunia when I struggled with sorrow or anger and felt better for it. Pug love it was.

I sat next to the young woman, seeing her eyes clearly for the first time, her glasses resting in her folded lap. They were hazel, but with brilliant bits of green and amber. She wore her hair back today, away from her narrow face, high cheekbones apparent. She really was pretty, though I felt a bit guilty I'd been judging her by traditional standards the way I had.

She watched me with a slowly growing smile until I looked away, blushing a bit. "Go ahead," she said. "You have questions."

I laughed, couldn't help it. "I'm known as the local busybody," I said, hating that Robert's dig felt so natural coming from my own lips. I could either despise it or embrace it, right? "Seems like people choose to die in my proximity before the compulsion to find out what happened takes me over and I turn into a bumbling sleuth who's a danger to herself and everyone around her."

It was Alice's turn to laugh. "That's not what I heard."

Huh? "I'm surprised," I said, slumping but hoping she might shine a light where darkness had settled. "I thought that was the general opinion around town." Okay, well, maybe Crew and Robert, Vivian. I was being a bit harsh. Didn't mean her alternative story wasn't welcome at a time when I could really use a pep talk.

"According to Oliver," she said, "you've solved three murders the police wouldn't have been able to crack without you."

Well now. Not just a glimmer of hope, but full out ego stroking time, was it? Yes, I wasn't above letting her ease me into feeling better, truth or no truth. And I could return the favor, just in case we were sharing a headspace as well as a bench and a pug's adoring grin between us.

"Looks like we have something in common," I said. "According to your blog you've exposed a lot of frauds the police wouldn't have been able to uncover without *you*." I purposely used the same language and she grinned.

"Looks that way," she said. And sighed, patting the gap in the bench. I had to help Petunia hoist herself up, but she settled with happy contentment, her head on Alice's lap, leaving me with the fragrant end. Awesome. Alice stroked the pug's velvet ears as she spoke again, her humor still faint in the back of her tone but more weariness than anything showing through. "It wasn't something I chose to do," she said. "It just kind of…"

"Happened." I nodded, feeling a bubbling of kinship grow for her. "I hear you, sister." Crap happened to me all the time. Far too often. Not my fault, right?

Her quick smile faded again. "I've been trying for years to finally get someone to listen before she vanished again." She lost me a moment before my mind translated Alice referred to Sadie. Frustration, old hurt, too, in those words, in the tightening of her forehead, though her fingers remained soft on Petunia's fur. As if she'd detached her body from her mind. "And now it's too late."

"Though, in the end, it's a win, isn't it?" Not a nice way to succeed and really a dark offer of comfort. I had to try better next time. "She's gone. She can't lie to anyone else." Yeah, not much better than the first effort. I wasn't very good at the whole tact and class thing, apparently.

Alice nodded despite my awkwardness, looked up, exhaled heavily. "There should be satisfaction in her death, Fee." She flinched then, caught my eyes. "I didn't mean it that way. I didn't want her dead." Cool, we were equally awkward. I'd keep her. Alice paused before shrugging. "Okay, there were a few times I wished she'd just... but I didn't kill her."

"We're not sure anyone did, just yet," I said. Why did my mind always assume murder?

Alice's lips twitched. "Because you believe in coincidence."

Okay, there was that. Not just me again, huh? I really had found a soul sister. "Oh, absolutely," I said.

We laughed together, though with little humor despite the growing trust I felt for her.

"I'm worried more so about the technology she used," Alice said then. "It's so advanced. I've never seen anything like it. If it becomes the standard for her kind, I'm afraid doing my job is going to get harder."

Her kind, like Sadie was another race all together. "Her grandson, Denver," I said, "has to be the source."

She bit her lower lip, her hand pausing on Petunia's ear, a fact that the pug protested with a soft groan and a wiggle. Alice began again, the dog falling still while she spoke. "That's what I was thinking." We shared a secret smile and for a moment I felt like a little kid making a new friend.

"Maybe someone should have a talk with him. A firm talk. About ethics." I still wanted to find out why he felt the need to apologize to Pamela. To uncover what happened that made my friend assault Sadie ten years ago.

"Maybe two people should." Alice wrinkled her nose, met my eyes a long moment before she spoke again. "I usually work alone. But this is your town. I'd like to offer that option. From one busybody to another."

I snorted. This was hilarious. And yet, I was considering it, wasn't I? Oh yes. Yes, I was. Because I'd never had a partner in snoop before.

"This is a terrible idea," I said. "I'm in."

CHAPTER NINETEEN

WE HEADED FOR THE house together, Petunia waddling between us while I did my best not to back out of what I'd just agreed to. Thing was, talking to Denver didn't have to connect with Sadie's death. I could just chat with him, right? Poor kid lost his grandmother. I didn't have to go into the conversation with a motive. I was just going to trail along with Alice. She'd do all the busybodying.

I'd gotten really good at lying to myself.

But when I walked into the kitchen, found Mom serving Emelia tea at the counter, the woman's tears increasing at the sight of Alice, my budding partnership ended with her nodding quickly to me before hurrying out and into the main house. I let her go, joining Mom and the grieving mother who had, apparently, changed her mind about coming downstairs.

At least it seemed my own mom was over her bad mood. Or was doing a great job hiding it from the weeping woman. When she met my eyes, hers were a bit guarded, but at least she wasn't pissed off anymore that I could tell. Good to know for later, if Mom's attitude shift was going to reoccur. Giving her someone to nurture flipped her switch.

Fee. You did not just come up with a plan to manipulate your own mother. Bad daughter.

"I know I'm going to lose him." Emelia sobbed into a tissue Mom handed her.

"Amos?" Way to state the obvious. I quickly covered my blurtiness. "I'm sure that's not—"

"We fight all the time now." I don't think she even heard me, but explained why she was here despite his lunch delivery. They must have had words. "He wants me to let go of Manuel but I j-j-just can't." That last word was a wail that made Petunia whimper.

After the conversation I'd had with him earlier, I knew she was right.

"Of course you can't." Mom went for denial instead, rubbing small circles in the middle of Emelia's back. "He was your son. It's totally understandable you're struggling, Emelia."

"Amos doesn't see it that way." Mom's calm and support seemed to be helping. The woman wiped at her face, sighed deeply, even smiled just a little. "Thank you so much for being here for me, Lucy. You barely know me. But it's been wonderful being able to talk to you." She turned abruptly and grasped my hand in a steely grip. "You have a wonderful mother. I hope you never take her for granted."

Mom's eyes narrowed ever so slightly but her expression stayed level. Okay then. So she was feeling unappreciated was she? Thanks to something Vivian said? Or was she realizing something entirely new about her life Emelia brought to light? I'd take care of whatever I could do to help ease Mom's mind ASAP. More manipulation tactics were clearly in order.

"Amos went for a walk," Emelia abruptly changed the subject, her tone dropping to flat and dull. "To clear his head. But I know this trip was his last straw. I need to find out what happened to my son."

Not much I could say about that, nor Mom, either, though her murmured comfort seemed to improve things. Though, as the kitchen door swung open and Crew entered, I wondered if Mom's careful comforting was about to be shattered into a million pieces.

His gaze flickered to me a moment, but he addressed Emelia as she turned and gulped, a soft hiccup escaping her.

"Sheriff," she said. "How much longer do we have to stay here?"

He nodded to Mom before answering without even a simple gesture in kind for me. Wow, whatever, Crew Turner. "I'm still waiting on a tox report from the examiner's office," he said. "I'm sorry, Dr. Cortez, but I have more questions."

Amos joined us, face tight as he entered the kitchen in a rush. "Don't say anything, Emelia. We're done answering your questions, Sheriff, at least without legal representation."

Emelia gasped softly, one hand extending toward her husband. "Amos, it's all right."

"No, it's not." He crossed his arms over his chest. "We have rights. And with no proof of any kind of wrongdoing he can't hold us here."

Crew's jaw jumped but he sounded cool and professional enough when he answered. "It's a request, Mr. Cortez. I simply wanted to go over your statements to make sure nothing new came up."

Amos hesitated while his wife shrugged.

"We have nothing to hide," she said. "Perhaps a more private location?" She stood, wavered a little, faint smile for Mom, a hand squeeze between friends. And then she left the kitchen, striding past her husband and Crew. Amos followed her, glaring at the sheriff who exhaled like he wanted to comment before he spun back, index finger jabbing at me.

"Don't even think about it," he said, before stomping off after them.

"Screw you," I muttered before turning to Mom. "Seriously, what is his problem?"

Yeah, forgot she was still mad at me for some undetermined reason around what I was guessing had to do with taking her for granted.

"Just stay out of it, Fee, why don't you?" I'd never seen Mom so exasperated. She turned her back on me and began to fill the dishwasher more firmly than necessary while I bit my tongue and left the room.

The lunch guests were gone, the dining room

empty. Instead of lingering in the foyer, knowing if I did I'd work up the kind of steam that would end up with me confronting Mom. But not the sort of confrontation that led to amicable hugging and crying and telling each other we loved one another, but the type that instead devolved into a shouting match where we were both sobbing for the wrong reason after saying things neither of us really meant.

Phew. Giant thoughts there, but I knew I was right.

Instead, I took the smarter (cowardly?) route and got out of Petunia's, taking my pug with me since she'd had a sorry experience herself this morning with my mother and her temper. There'd be time to sort out what was going on with Mom when I wasn't so fired up about Crew. I stomped through the chill afternoon air, leaves crunching underfoot on the sidewalk, Petunia happy to toddle along at my side all the way to the news office.

I forced myself to admire the decorations in people's yards, to think happier thoughts instead of the cranky ones that had begun to sour my newfound sense of self. We were two days out from Halloween and I realized I still needed to stock up on treats. Last year I'd miscalculated and not bought nearly enough, saved by Mom and her caramel popcorn skills. But I didn't want her to have to come rushing to my aid this year. Something she did a lot of the last little while, I had to admit, and not just because the ladies weren't working. Mom was there for me no matter what I needed and I really had been taking advantage of that. Not that she'd seemed to mind all along, but.

But. I sighed out my temper, knowing it had nothing to do with my mother. If anything, I knew I owed her a huge hug and an apology. Ultimately, she was right. Alice's offer would have to be kindly turned down. I really needed to stop, once and for all. This was none of my business.

Keep telling yourself that, Fee. Maybe it'll kick in eventually.

I purposely stopped outside the bakery this time, noting the news office door was still closed, the lights out anyway, so it wasn't like I could even talk to Pamela if I wanted to. Instead I marched into French's with my mother's change of attitude in mind, Petunia's acute attention to the smells inside triggering a wriggling excited dance.

Whoops. Forgot about her stomach and her utter focus on anything food related. Instead of letting her stop me, I went to the counter, peeking over the shoulder of the next person in line. But Vivian was nowhere in sight.

Right. She wouldn't be working the counter. Much to Petunia's dismay, I dragged her back out and onto the street, circling into the driveway next to the shop. Spotted the bright red convertible with the hard top installed for fall, knew at least this conversation could happen today and needing the outlet for my anger, quite frankly.

The back door gaped, the kitchen on the other side, just the person I was looking for stepping out into the alley at the exact moment I came to a stomping halt, scowling at her as she froze in place, staring back.

"I'll only tell you once," I snarled. "Stay out of my place and away from my mother."

Faint annoyance flickered over her face. "Mind your own business, Fanny," she said in that dismissive tone that dug pinpricks of fury deep under my skin.

"I mean it, Vivian," I snapped back, blocking her way but not touching her. She huffed an impatient sigh, flicking her blonde hair over her shoulder, designer wool coat catching strands and forcing her to stroke them away with one angry hand.

"Fine, whatever. Since you say so." She arched an eyebrow, sarcasm so thick I could walk on it. "Can I go now?"

I should have just stepped aside, message delivered, and got over her already. Should have taken her at her word and called it a win.

Should have done a lot of things. Instead, in true Fiona Fleming fashion, I lost my crap and let it out on her.

I don't remember what I said next, and it doesn't really matter, because it was clear from her reaction she was spoiling for a fight, too. We spent the next two or three minutes that felt like forever shouting at each other as if we were kids on a playground calling names, though neither of us stooped to hair pulling or scratching. I considered it, don't get me wrong. Would have been so satisfying to yank on that perfect blonde hair just once. But I really needed to vent and Vivian was the ideal target to get it all out with.

I finally did step aside as she clomped past me on her high heeled boots, all elegance missing while she fumbled with her car door twice before jerking it open, throwing in her handbag, tossing a final round of swearwords at me before her last line made it through loud and clear.

"You're a menace to Reading, Fiona Fleming," she snarled. "And everyone around you. Four murders since you came home, think about that." I grunted in shock at her remark. Not my fault! She didn't stop to let me protest. "And you're in the middle of all of them. There are people in this town who wish you'd just go the hell back to New York City and take your terrible luck with you!"

With that, she threw herself inside and gunned the engine. I let her peel off, panting, throat sore from yelling, realizing only then a trio of faces stared, white and shocked, out the back door.

The moment her staff saw me notice them they slammed it behind them, leaving me to shake and snarl a few more choice curses at the pavement at my feet before I drew a deep breath and let the last of my anger go.

At least no one called the cops. That would have been the worst, to have Robert show up with his lights flashing. Worse, to have Crew appear and make a bigger mess. I forced myself to retreat, to make for home again, head down, not wanting to see if there were more witnesses, positive there had to be. We were downtown, in the core of Reading, after all.

And I'd cut loose in a pretty public way. Which meant in about an hour everyone in town who didn't know Vivian and I just had a shouting match behind the bakery would have all the details.

Loved small town life. Seriously.

It did a lot to settle my head, though, I'd give the whole childish outburst that. I felt better, if embarrassed by my lack of control, my thoughts about Mom even guiltier that I'd not shown her the kind of support and appreciation she'd done for me. And the fact I honestly did need to mind my own business wasn't lost on me at all.

Time to go home and hug my mom and start a new chapter for Fiona Fleming.

Except, of course, the sight of Oliver Watters entering the front door of his antique shop across the street made me stop.

Pivot.

And go after him before I could stop myself.

CHAPTER TWENTY

I MADE IT ACROSS the street without getting hit by a car, so bonus points for actually flinging myself into the roadway and having luck on my side. Petunia panted next to me, her anxiety clear as I dragged her into the antique store, the darkness of the interior and musty smell washing me over with a rather gloomy mix that triggered my bad mood all over again.

I almost turned around and walked away. This was dumb. I'd just agreed to stop digging into things that had nothing to do with me. In fact, I had already begun to pivot, sneaker squeaking on the old tile, when Oliver appeared out of the dimness of the interior of his shop, coat still on, hair standing up at odd angles like a brush was the least of his possessions.

"Miss Fleming," he said. "Can I help you?" Not that he sounded like he really had any interest in being helpful, but he asked and that was enough for my brain to seize my mouth and open it and speak before I could shut myself up and just leave already.

Story of my life.

"What's your history with Sadie Hatch?" I guess civility and subtlety had left the building without saying goodbye. I held my ground despite my sudden nervousness I'd pushed his buttons too far too fast in my own need to stop feeling like I was doing something wrong.

Didn't help my case any. His bushy eyebrows came together immediately, scowl jerking at his wrinkled mouth. He stormed toward me, waving his hands in front of him like he was shooing a pest out of his trash at 2AM.

"I've heard about you and your poking around," he said. "Not this time, missy. Out. Out! Before I call the sheriff and have him throw you out."

I wish I could say I went quietly and peacefully with decorum and the kind of self-respect that was due someone my age. Instead, I flailed a little back at him, stumbling as I backpedaled, hitting the glass door with my butt and stepping on Petunia's toes. She squealed out a sharp yip of protest that made me jerk in response while Oliver closed the distance, forcing me out on to the street by his approach, my squirming and now frightened pug lunging against the end of her leash, pulling me even further off balance.

I found myself on the sidewalk, the door slammed firmly shut in my face, sign turned as he glared at me, lock clicking over. I glared right back, shaking from the sudden surge of adrenaline, knowing I'd made a further mess that hadn't been necessary and without any kind of plan to make it right.

One thing burned in my head as I led Petunia home, her quick looks up at me almost constant as we made our way. The comment he'd made, how he'd heard about me. Alice said differently, had twisted his opinion away from the rather pleasant alternative she'd suggested and drove it home very clearly she'd been trying to be nice. Or recruit me in to her own investigation by making me think the whole town didn't consider me a nuisance.

The biggest problem with his verbal attack? It

mirrored enough what Robert's fumbling attempt to make me feel bad began, what Crew's continual commands and Vivian's parting shot improved on substantially. I was a bit of a disaster by the time I led Petunia up the steps to the B&B, doing my best not to dissolve into poor me tears, the lighthearted renewal of myself long gone.

I spent the rest of the afternoon to myself, keeping my head down, helping Mom as best I could with tea before escaping upstairs to do some cleaning when the Cortez's went out for a walk. Alice was nowhere around, and just as well. I would likely have broken down and told her in no uncertain terms I just couldn't help her. Instead, I found my way down to my apartment and huddled there for a bit, hugging Petunia and trying to pull myself together.

The longer I sat there, nighttime closing in, deepening the shadows in my living room when I failed to turn on the lights, the more resentful I felt. I was *not* bad luck. Every death in this town happened because other people were jerks to each other. Pete Wilkins was killed by his own great aunt, for goodness sake, hardly anything to do with me. And Mason Patterson was a total dick. Not that he deserved to die, but I didn't even know the guy, not like Jenny Markham who took her own twisted revenge. As for Skip Anderson, if he hadn't been such a selfish ass and driven that kid to suicide, he'd still be alive.

My proximity to Sadie's end was all wrong place, wrong time. Vivian could suck it. Oliver, too. Crew Turner? The jury was still out on how I felt about that.

It would have been the smart thing to do, to have a shower, get into bed, watch TV, forget all of this. Instead, I flipped open my laptop and did a search for Denver Hatch.

Found his social media, his about page listing him as a student at MIT. Computer programming. Gotcha. But it was October. Why wasn't he at school?

I closed the lid, realizing full dark had descended, hearing the house above me settle into quiet. I couldn't let this go. I wouldn't. It felt like failure, just huddling here in the basement, as if I had done something wrong. So maybe investigating crimes that really should have been left to the police wasn't exactly right, but on the other hand, I'd helped, I'd really made a difference. I just wanted answers. Just to talk to Denver and find out what he knew about

Pamela. That was all.

Knowing instead I was doing exactly what I'd regret later, I changed into black jeans and a dark sweater, slipping upstairs and out the back door, Mom long gone, Dad, too. The side gate still hadn't been fixed, but that served me tonight. It was a short jaunt to Sadie's, while my mind whirled, made a plan. I would walk up to the front door, knock. Smile at Denver. Ask him politely and kindly what he knew. Simple, straight forward. Not intruding, just asking. He could answer or not, but at least I'd have tried.

The notion of calling Crew and telling him Denver had information did cross my mind. Except of course past history told me he'd either yell at me—I'd had enough yelling for today, thank you— and tell me to mind my own business—so tired of hearing that—or sigh like I'd ruined his life, and then, repetitiveness redux, tell me to mind my own business. Any combination of, "Fee, no, stop, go home," and so on, etc., ad nauseam.

I reached Sadie's house, paused at the walkway. Did I really want to do this? There weren't any lights on, the place dark from what I could see. Maybe Denver wasn't even home. My feet were moving, carrying me forward and toward the front door when

I noticed illumination flickering inside, suspiciously like a flashlight. Someone beat me here.

Likely Alice. Though it could also be the killer. If there *was* a killer. I really had to stop jumping to conclusions, too. Right?

Right.

I climbed the steps, wincing when they creaked, looking behind me and realized the street was completely blocked from this point. I couldn't see out and no one could see me creeping Sadie's place. Well, there was that, at least. Though I had zero doubt if I was spotted Crew would be here in a flash when he found out. That meant I had a very short period of time to make a choice.

Knock or sneak?

When the flashlight flickered in the window of the door, I dodged its beam and drew a breath. Raised my hand to knock, caught myself grasping the knob instead. Imagine my surprise when it turned easily and silently under my hand.

And that's how I found myself breaking and entering on a crime scene. At least I had company, if the flashlight wielder already inside—who had either picked the lock or also found the house open—was any defense. I closed the door behind me, mind squealing that this was the worst possible idea I'd ever had in my entire life and what the hell was wrong with me right now. Worse even than finding myself hiding under a desk while someone I suspected in a murder case was this close to uncovering me where I wasn't supposed to be.

Thinking about former head nurse and administrator Ruth Wilkins wasn't helping any. Nor did it stop me, though, did it? I followed the dark shape lurking inside, flashlight a beacon as it passed out of the entry and into the dining room, heart pounding, breathing through my parted lips as silently as possible, pausing when the intruder—um, I was an intruder, too, remember?—hesitated. Before the person spun around and shone the light directly in my eyes.

It only lasted a second, long enough for my fear to spike, for me to meep a little, before the figure rushed to my side and grasped my elbow in one hand.

"Fee," Alice whispered, the faint glow of her light shining off her glasses. "You're here!"

Um, duh. "What are you doing? This is illegal." I had zero right to comment on what was legal and what wasn't. Though I could claim that I saw the intruder and followed her. Except Crew would argue I should have just called him. That whole scenario ending with him shouting at me in his office and threatening to arrest me spun out in a matter of seconds while Alice shrugged.

"I'm not taking anything," she said. "I just wanted a look at the system. And I've been watching the house all day. No one's home."

So Denver hadn't come back here. I noticed there wasn't any crime scene tape up and there hadn't been any on the front door. Had Crew gotten the tox screen back and it really was a heart attack?

I deflated suddenly, feeling like an idiot. I'd turned myself into knots and made a mountain out of a molehill. Kind of relieved and embarrassed to jump to conclusions where there were none to make, I accepted I'd been a jerk and this time decided for sure, 100%, I was done being nosy.

At the exact moment Alice grasped my arm and screamed as the ghost of an old woman appeared right in front of us.

CHAPTER TWENTY-ONE

I ADMIT I SCREAMED too, a combined reaction, part nervousness for my illegal break and enter and part expenditure of extra energy I'd been feeding with my angst the last few hours. Alice grabbed for me and I grabbed right back and the pair of us shrieked like co-eds in a bad horror movie as the stationary image of my Grandmother Iris glared at us in all her glowing, rigid glory.

Footsteps pounded overhead, someone racing down the stairs. I barely had time to shut off my panicked reaction when the light flared into life and the ghostly image disappeared. Denver stared at both of us with huge eyes, mouth gaping open and we stared in frozen dread right back.

I was expecting him to call Crew, to shout at us to get out, to do something along the lines that a normal person would do if he found two strangers snooping around his living room. Instead, Denver's eyes locked on Alice and he actually smiled in dazed surprise.

"I can't believe it," he said. "She told me you were coming, wouldn't let me be here because she thought I might..." he gulped, gesturing at the wall behind us with a small remote control before transferring it to his pocket and extended one hand. He seemed to think twice, rubbing the palm on his jeans hastily, fingers orange from some snack he'd been eating upstairs, obviously. Hiding out? "Sorry, there's still system glitches." He actually blushed. "Denver Hatch."

"Alice Moore," she said, smiling faintly, like she was supposed to be there, had an appointment, wasn't committing a B&E.

"Yes, I know." He was almost gushing, grinning at me, at her. "I follow your blog. Have for ages."

A fan. How convenient. Hopefully enough to keep him from calling Crew and having us arrested. Because Dad would kill me. Mom, too. And I'd never live it down.

Holy crap, what was I thinking?

I almost shook in relief, keeping my mouth shut while Alice responded with the kind of levelheadedness that I wished I possessed on the best of days.

"Thanks for reading," she said. "Do you have a favorite case?"

He rambled on a minute, her murmuring and nodding like this was some kind of convention and he was there for her autograph and not a late night break in. So awkward, but I was willing to let it unfold as long as I could just sneak out later with no one the wiser.

Alice had to go and ruin it, didn't she?

"This system you designed," she said, gesturing around her without a hint of judgment, "it's pretty remarkable. There were moments I was almost fooled. That says a lot for your skill."

Denver blanched, guilt flashing over his face. I was positive then we were cooked, that he was about to reach for the phone and the end of my life as I knew it, when he's fingers brushed his pocket, the remote a bulge inside it, and shrugged.

"I didn't build it for her," he said. "It's supposed to be a VR system I'm selling for gaming."

Alice smiled, nodded. "It's really amazing," she said. "You must have a huge amount of interest for it."

His grin came slowly back as his cheeks pinked, embarrassment no longer about helping his grandmother from what I could tell, but fed by her praise. "Kind of," he said. "Did you want to see how it works?"

Did I. Okay, so five seconds ago I just wanted to get out. Now, though? Now I couldn't wait to get a chance to find out what was behind the curtain. Because I was an idiot who couldn't keep her curiosity to herself.

I shouldn't have been surprised our little show and tell would have consequences. Denver was just moving, heading deeper into the dining room, when the front door banged open and Crew stormed in. How did I know it was Crew without seeing him? Intuition. Gut instinct, and terrible luck, after all.

Yup, there he was a moment later, frowning at us from the open pocket doors, hands landing on his hips, face tight with anger. "Tell me I'm not here to make two arrests."

I gulped, though I wasn't going to fight him if he had to take me in. I'd broken the law this time, hands down, no contest. A quick round of agreement and it would be all over, kaputski. I almost took a step toward him, mouth open to confess, when Denver spoke.

"Nice to see you, Sheriff," he said, sounding much more self-possessed than I gave him credit for. "I was about to call and invite you to join us." He gestured at Alice, at me. "I offered to show them the system I created that made my grandmother's business so popular." He grimaced while my guilt tried to poke me. But he hadn't exactly lied, right? Denver had just finished offering to do just that. Never mind we'd broken in first.

That could be swept under the rug if I could just keep my conscience from getting the better of me. From the scowl Crew leveled at me, he didn't believe it, not for a second. Made me wonder if I'd just ruined any chance I had to actually see where things might go between us. Shook myself for considering that at a time like this. And raised my chin to him so he would see I wasn't about to be intimidated either by his bossiness or his lack of mixed up attention.

So there.

Crew backed down, though I was sure he still didn't believe us. "What happened to you assuring me there was nothing to show me, Denver?" So the young man had stonewalled, had he? Crew seemed less irritated about Denver lying to him than he did seeing me in Sadie's dining room. "Does that mean the reports of two people breaking in were false, too, or can I trust anything you say?" Neighbors. So nosy.

Denver shrugged. "Do you want to see the setup or not?"

I had to hand it to the kid, he must have had a real backbone to stand up to Crew the way he did, and for two strangers, though it was likely his adoration of Alice had something to do with it.

"Fine," Crew grunted. "Do go on." He met my eyes again. "We'll discuss this further when you're done."

Okay, so for the last several days I'd been on this put your right hand in and shake it all about hokey pokey of an up and down thrill ride when it came to my emotions. I knew the source, stared part of it in the face at that moment, while my nervous guilt shifted once again to anger. Clearly I was in desperate need of therapy or drugs or some kind of shock treatment because I was losing my marbles one shiny little bit at a time. Instead of nodding to him, giving him the win and diffusing his anger, I felt my eyes tighten, my jaw jump in time with his.

He did *not* just threaten me.

Oh Fee. Sigh.

Denver was on the move again, enough so he distracted Crew from his little macho muscle flex of bravado that got him nowhere, the jerk. I turned away from him, molars aching from clenching them to find Denver crouching next to the head of the table while the lights went dim.

"It works on holographics," he said, tone brightening into happiness, and I understood why. Here was a chance to show off something he created, a truly amazing something as the image of my grandmother reappeared, hovering beside me. I reached out to her, touched her, saw her waver. Denver guided her with his controls around the table, even had her pass through the surface, the three dimensional rendering wavering and glowing but ghostly enough it still gave me chills.

"The system takes a static image and extrapolates three dimensions," he said. "Not perfectly, but enough to pass for this scenario." Another image flickered into life, this one that of Manuel Cortez. Except his smiling face, his static features, looked nothing like the ghostly apparition that flew through the doorway at us.

I didn't get to ask how he'd managed that because Alice was talking.

"The breeze and the sounds?" She turned in a slow circle. "I didn't see speakers."

"Embedded in the chair backs," he said, grinning, the light from the ghosts he summoned lighting his expression in a way that made him ghastly. "The breeze is generated through pinholes in the ceiling tiles." He pointed upward. "Small fans are quiet enough to keep the sound down but just enough to stir the air."

"Fascinating," she said, beaming at him. "This is truly remarkable."

"You harvest the images from social media." Crew didn't sound impressed.

Denver flinched, stood up, the system shutting down, lights returning as he pocketed his remote again. "My grandmother did," he said. "I programmed them from what she gave me."

"Sadie didn't have the kind of technical knowledge to dig up everything," I said. Softly, like I knew better than to speak even as I kicked myself for not keeping quiet. Denver was all that stood between me and a criminal charge, after all, but I couldn't help myself.

He sighed, sagged against the table. "I taught her how," he said. "At first, I just wanted the money to build the system. I didn't care what she was doing with what I gave her. Nothing illegal." He shook his head, but was he fooling himself? That part was definitely Crew's department. "At least, getting the info and images wasn't. I only used clean channels for that. It's amazing what you can find out about people, just out there, unprotected."

"And the rest?" Crew tilted his head, dark hair shadowing his blue eyes. He looked tired, but calm at least. "You didn't participate in the frauds?"

Denver shrugged. "I guess, in a way. I did the programming. But honestly, most of the people who paid her knew it wasn't real. This was supposed to be fun, you know? And a great way to test my system." He looked guilty all over again. "Except for folks like the Cortez's." He hesitated. "I told her I wasn't going to help her anymore when I heard the mother thought my grandma was a real psychic."

"I'm sure," Crew said, sarcasm too much for me.

"You said you've had interest in this tech, Denver," I said, cutting off the sheriff and knowing it would cost me later. Likely in yelling. But the kid was being forthcoming and he had more to tell. "Gaming companies?"

Again with the hesitation, this time accompanied by a tightening of his own jaw. Going around lately. "Maybe I need to talk to a lawyer first."

Um, huh?

"Let me guess," Crew said, taking a step forward, accusation in everything about him, including his stance, his grim expression, his tone and, ultimately, his words. "You wanted to sell it for big bucks but your grandmother wanted to keep her little secret weapon to herself."

Denver flinched. Right on target. If I was going to be fair about it, more than enough motive for murder.

"Except there's no proof Sadie was murdered or that her death was foul play," I said out loud because I was an idiot who had zero control over herself.

Crew's scowl told me to shut up while Denver spoke.

"Truth is," he said, "I had already sold the system. She just found out last night, a few hours before…" he stopped, seemed to shake himself. "Before you all showed up." He ran one hand through his hair. "I didn't want to betray her, she was the only family I had left." He swallowed hard, stared at the floor, trembling all over. Alice went to him, held his hand and he looked startled for a moment before he relaxed and finished directly to her. "We fought. It was awful. I stormed out, didn't want to be here. Figured I'd dismantle the setup after you all had gone. It was the last night she was going to have access to the system. I owed her that much for taking me in when my parents died. But I was done letting her use it to hurt people."

Alice nodded, smiled faintly, kindly, while my brain told me he should have trusted his instincts and waited to have a lawyer present. From the look on Crew's face, he was about to drop a bombshell I'd known all along and just didn't have the courage to stick to.

"Considering your grandmother was murdered," the sheriff said, "I'm going to have to ask you to come down to the station and give me that statement in a more formal setting."

CHAPTER TWENTY-TWO

I GLARED AT THE sheriff with my temper and protectiveness combining into a big ball of righteousness. "You knew this whole time. Why didn't you say anything?" I turned to Denver, shook my head abruptly. "Don't say another word, just stay quiet." He looked startled, pale while Alice held his hand. "You asked for a lawyer, Denver." I met Alice's eyes, hoped she got my meaning. "We heard you ask." Technically he hadn't. But screw Crew Turner right now for trying to trap this kid into saying more than he'd wanted to in the first place. Alice understood my message, obviously, because she nodded back.

"Absolutely, that's what I heard," she said. "This

is entrapment, Sheriff."

"So nothing you've said is admissible in any way." I spun on Crew, crossing my arms over my chest. I shouldn't have been defending the kid. He was a suspect in his grandmother's murder. But he'd played me honest not so long ago, had my back when he could have thrown me to the wolves. Something about him told me he wasn't guilty. That at the very least Denver deserved fair treatment.

I think Crew was about two shakes from a stroke, he was so mad. I am positive if we'd been alone he would have lost his crap completely and likely yelled at me so loudly the fight with Vivian in the back alley at the bakery would be a whispering nothing compared to the level of volume he'd be able to muster.

Instead, face so tense the vein in his forehead stuck out in alarming relief on his dark red complexion, he spun on one heel and left the room. Stomped through the entry. Opened and then slammed the front door. Was gone a long, quiet moment while the three of us waited for something, anything, to happen.

When nothing did, I was positive his head blew up and he was out there, lying on the grass, a stump all that remained like some cartoon character who'd exploded for a punch line. Not the nicest visual to have to process, and more than enough to make me worry for Crew's physical safety tied to the guilt I might have killed him.

I'd never, ever live it down.

I shouldn't have let my imagination run off with me or been concerned for his welfare. He returned a few seconds later, the door closing behind him firmly but without the same house-shaking force, footsteps not so much stomping as striding. When he appeared in the doorway, he looked much calmer in appearance but clearly at the end of his rope.

"Denver," he said, voice crackling though he kept it down, "please, come down to the station in the morning to make a statement. And have a lawyer with you." He shot me a glare that told me if I opened my mouth again in that particular moment in time he'd arrest me for nothing and throw away the key and not care even a little bit about the law.

Message received.

Denver looked at Alice who nodded encouragement. "I will," he said. "But answer me this." He must have known the sheriff wasn't in the mood, so kudos again for bravery. Though, maybe it was just me who triggered the kind of over-the-top frustrated reaction that made the sheriff so nuts. Probably. When Crew didn't blow up, just stood there, I sadly accepted that was the truth while Denver forged on. "How did she die?" His lower lip trembled just a little, voice catching when he visibly fought his emotions. "What killed her?"

Crew was quiet a long moment, like he didn't want to answer. When he finally spoke, there was real empathy in his voice. "I'm sorry, I didn't mean to tell you this way." Another glare at me. Oh, sure, blame me for screwing up your job, Mr. Sheriff Crappy Pants. I was apparently out of clever comebacks, even in my own head. "The tox screen found poison in her system. It triggered a heart attack."

"The tea?" I shut up instantly after blurting those two words.

Denver frowned, shaking his head. "Store bought," he said. "Just generics that she took from cheap bags and mixed herself to make it sound fancy."

Was nothing about this woman real? Seriously.

"I'm still investigating," Crew said. "But everyone here that night has more questions to answer now that I know it was foul play." Another glare? Really,

Crew? Had he also run out of anything but that nasty expression to communicate with?

"Denver," I said, "what was the connection between Oliver and Sadie?" Might as well ask everything while I was here and now, right? Crew needed to know, after all.

Her grandson seemed perplexed. "I don't know," he said, while Alice held very still next to him, refusing to meet my eyes.

Telling me that she knew exactly what was between them and was keeping it to herself.

I was surprised to find myself on the sidewalk in front of Sadie's house a minute later, further questions unasked. Alice remaining behind to talk with the excited Denver while Crew stood with his back to me, facing his truck, not moving. He'd left ahead of me after another firm request Denver see him first thing, stomping out, clearly still agitated. One look at the bush next to the front door, roots exposed where someone grabbed it and partially uprooted it from the ground, told me what Crew had done in the few seconds he'd taken when he'd left us alone. I bit my lower lip, wishing things had gone differently, feeling badly about the mess I was making of our relationship.

And by relationship I meant our constant head butting over dead bodies punctuated by brief moments of maybe he was a nice guy after all smothered in stay out of it, Fiona.

Complicated. Naturally.

I hesitated when I spotted him standing there, not wanting to make things worse but unable to move past him without bumping into him. He'd planted himself firmly in the middle of the sidewalk and though I could have tucked against the fence it would have been very apparent I did so to avoid him. Avoiding him wasn't getting me anywhere.

"Fee." He spoke my name as I paused to try to find the words to say to either get him to move or soften his anger. Both if I could help it. The tone of it sent a shiver through me. Not furious as I expected. Disappointed. Like I'd let him down. It silenced any protest I could have offered, any anger, smothering it in guilt as he went on, back rigid, still not looking at me. "I know full well you broke in here tonight." He stopped for a breath, like saying it took the air from his lungs while I clenched inside and held quiet. "And I also know full well you honestly think you're helping. That you more than likely can't stop yourself. It's in you. The need to know. The detective's soul." His shoulders bowed slightly before stiffening again while I stared at the back of his head, mouth gaping open, heart hurting. "Fee, I *know*. I get it." He turned around then, finally facing me, expression far harder than his voice. "But you have to stop. Just stop. Or go get training. Because you're killing me, here."

I had nothing to say. Agreeing wouldn't help. Neither would arguing. Maybe he knew it. Instead of waiting for a response, he turned again and got in his truck, drove off without another word or acknowledgment. Leaving me to walk slowly home, feeling just about the lowest I ever had in my life. Even more than when I found out Ryan cheated, than when I thought I lost Petunia's to Pete. Those events triggered enough anger to smother my initial regret. Tonight, though?

Guilt and me were on our own.

It would have been so much easier if he'd just yelled. Better that then knowing I'd let him down in a way that he just couldn't take anymore.

There was a message waiting from Jared on my landline when I got home, but I was too tired to call. I found a note left behind from Mom I missed earlier, stuck to the fridge. The contents perked me a little.

Exciting news. Super secret project for Aundrea and Pamela. Vivian's going to be pissed. Love you, sorry about today. See you tomorrow. Mom.

Huh. Well, whatever it was, I was just glad my mother had a happy focus to shake her out of her funk. Because mine was deeper than ever.

With the Cortez's quiet in their room, I did a final tour of the house, missing Alice as she snuck into her own and closed the door behind her before I could say hello. I let her have her privacy, not in the mood for more questioning anyway. Besides, I had guests coming tomorrow, was prepped physically but not even remotely ready for them mentally or emotionally. At least Petunia was her happy go lucky self, happy to see me, though her mood shifted with mine and she plodded without any pep in her step as I went to the kitchen door to lock it.

And found Emelia at the counter, waiting for me. With tears on her face but rage there, too.

CHAPTER TWENTY-THREE

"IT'S TRUE, THEN," SHE said, leaving me stunned and a bit flatfooted to be honest, with no idea what she was talking about. "She was murdered."

Ah, Sadie. Okay. Why did that make Emelia mad again? I opened my mouth to reply when she stood and began pacing, anger better than sorrow, at least. "Amos was right. She was a fraud. Why else would someone kill her? Making me an utter fool for believing a thing she said."

Oh dear. "I'm afraid so." Winced at the cross-meaning. "I didn't mean you were a fool." She waved that off as I rushed on. "But I do believe she was killed because she was a fake." I watched the tall woman's face crumple while she sank onto the stool again.

"She was so convincing." She shook her head, hands heavy in her lap, but at least the anger—and the debilitating grief—seemed to have lifted from her, if only temporarily. "I've ruined myself, my credibility, ended friendships and alienated my husband. For what?"

"We want to believe so badly sometimes," I said, doing my best to say what I thought Mom might. "Anyone who judges you for wanting answers has no idea what you're going through." Yeah, that sounded very Lucy to me.

Emelia accepted my attempt to comfort her, so I must have hit the mark. "Thank you. You have all been so kind. But it's time for me to accept that I've been searching for answers that may never appear, certainly not at the hands of a lying woman who was clearly taking advantage of me. Amos is right. I need to find a way to let my son go." Funny how she said "my son" like that. Grief made us forget there were other people hurting, I guess. Like her husband who also lost his child. Emelia hugged herself, a bit of her grief back but likely it was habitual now instead of that true authentic rawness of a gaping, fresh wound.

I hoped it wouldn't take her over again. "She just knew so many things. Things no one else should have known."

"Things she could have uncovered with access to his social media?" I sat next to her.

"I suppose, for the most part. Except she knew Manuel wasn't—" She stopped suddenly, met my eyes with horror vaguely shining in her own before she clamped her lips together.

Manuel wasn't what?

Maybe I could have convinced her to tell me what she was about to spill if her husband hadn't appeared at the door. Amos looked tired, angry, but when Emelia turned toward him, her face crumpling, her arms out, he seemed surprised.

"Darling," she said, "I'm so sorry. Can you forgive me for being so blind?"

For a moment it seemed he wasn't willing, that the damage had, indeed, been done. Until he closed the distance and hugged her warmly, so much drama in the moment it was like I was living in someone else's romance novel.

I left them to their embrace, Amos murmuring into her hair, Emelia crying, but this time without the choking, sobbing sound that I'd heard from her before. Maybe they'd finally get to move on at last. I paused at my door, thinking about her. Was it an act? No, I couldn't believe that. But, my mind whispered. If Emelia found out when she got here that Sadie had lied to her... her grief was a powerful thing. Could she have killed the old woman in misguided revenge?

Silly. Chasing shadows and hints of nothing when I knew better. Except there had been three other deaths where my intuition finally led me to the truth. I had to stop myself halfway to the basement and inhale, exhale. Forced myself to remember the sound of Crew's voice, the hurt in him that I'd let him down. Did I care? Yes, I did. Because I cared about him.

That's why I went to bed and fell asleep and had nothing else to do with the murder of Sadie Hatch.

Yeah, um. Ahem. Not quite. Shocker, right?

That's why I went to bed with my laptop and researched the death of Manuel Cortez. While alarm bells went off in my head and an epiphany I'd already had the pieces to made me gasp. Emelia said it, but only now did I put together that the kid died of sudden heart failure while playing piano in a concert. He collapsed as he finished the last piece of the evening, while the applause for his performance swelled and the curtain fell.

Coincidence that the circumstances were far too close for comfort to the death of Sadie?

And, if so, was I right about Emelia after all?

Needless to say, I didn't get any sleep that night. Despite my lack of rest, I was up at my usual time, let Petunia out, ran my morning routine on autopilot while my mind continued to go around and around and around before landing on the same question, Emelia's little slip the night before she had stopped herself from finishing.

Sadie knew Manuel what?

Mom and Dad arrived at seven and after I hugged my mother, her beaming smile back in place, I let her breeze off to the kitchen before cornering Dad in the sitting room and telling him everything. Including, with wincing internal nervousness, about the break in.

I was positive he'd blow a gasket. Except, since he'd retired Dad seemed to have mellowed a lot, grinned at me like it was funny, especially when I told him Denver backed me and Alice without lying.

"That must have pissed Crew off," he chuckled.

"Dad." I smacked him in the chest. "I broke the

law."

"Sweetie," he said, poking me back, "you got away with it. Keep going."

True. Didn't make it right. I was actually offended by his attitude, but finished my story, ending with the statement I couldn't seem to shake, the similarity in Manuel's death to Sadie's, while Dad nodded, now grim and secretive.

"I was coming to the same conclusion," he said.

"You knew?" He could have told me.

"I figured you'd have checked out the kid's death by now ono your own." Dad shrugged, no biggie. Honestly, I'd planned to, just hadn't gotten to it until last night. He knew me too well. I was his daughter, after all, and blaming him for this need I had to solve mysteries might not cut it with Crew, but it made me feel better. Standing there in the sun filled front room with my grinning, dare I say proud Dad actually approving of this turn of events, I let myself unclench from the horrible knot I'd wound myself into over Crew.

I was who I was. If Crew didn't like it. Well.

Dating sites. Right.

"Could this be connected to Manuel?" Thinking out loud didn't seem to bother Dad. "Was he some kind of collateral damage? Or was Sadie?" I was grasping straws here. Emelia had a secret, her son had one, too. And that made her a suspect.

"I made a call yesterday to an old buddy of mine," he said. "I'll let you know what I hear. Hopefully today."

Well, this was new. "Why the sudden change in attitude, Dad?"

He paused a long moment before shrugging. "I can't change you, kid. Wouldn't want to, either. You're damned good at this. So am I, turns out." He winked. "Let's be done minding our own business."

Um, okay, what? Dad hugged me, kissed the top of my head and left me there, far too cheery for someone who should have been mad at his only daughter for breaking the law he upheld to the letter for so many years.

On the other hand, had he? How much did I know about how Dad did business? I shuddered at the thought he didn't play straight, that my father might have been... no, not saying it in my head, even. Because no one in the world was perfect, and everyone had some kind of dirt on their hands. Thinking about Malcolm made me pause all over again.

I couldn't do this right now. Maybe not ever.

I was saved further contemplation by the front door and Pamela Shard. She slipped into the foyer like a guilty woman looking for sanctuary, spotting me and freezing in place, her face pale, her eyes huge. Petunia waddled over to her, breaking her moment of indecision. Pamela bent and stroked the pugs ears before coming slowly to my side, her face drawn and tired, eyes sad.

"I need to talk to you," she said. "Fee, I think I'm in serious trouble."

CHAPTER TWENTY-FOUR

I DREW HER TO me, sat her on the sofa, held her hands while she trembled next to me. Her normally precise bob was in disarray, makeup long gone from her eyes, her suit exchanged for a t-shirt and jeans, sneakers. She looked like hell and was honestly scaring me just then.

Did she kill Sadie? And if she confessed to me, what was I going to do about it?

I almost called for Dad, just to have backup, when Pamela spoke.

"My grandparents lived in Iowa." I had no idea. "I moved there to be with them when Granddad got sick." She stared at the floor rather than meet my eyes, clearly lost in memory. "It was easier to go, to leave when Aundrea's family forced her to marry that beast, Pete Wilkins." I knew this part already but didn't say anything. Waited for her to go on. She fetched a tissue from one pocket and used it to dab at her nose. "I had school, was busy, did my best, Fee. But when Granddad died, my grandmother kind of lost it." Fair enough. "They'd been together for almost fifty years. She just wanted to say goodbye." She looked up at last, met my gaze, hers full of tears. "She'd gone home that night, kissed him, said she'd see him in the morning. I talked her into leaving, just once. That night." She sobbed, a short, sad sound. "And he died."

Now I was crying, too. "I'm sorry." I managed that much at least.

She shook her head, hair whipping violently around her cheeks. "It doesn't matter now. It was a long time ago. Thing was, she didn't blame me. But she wanted to see him one more time. So she started looking."

"Psychics." Made sense.

"She started staying up late, couldn't sleep. I'd find her watching silly infomercials for hours at a time, just to keep herself from thinking. Then, one night, a show came on, about psychics contacting the dead. Whatever it was that triggered her, from that moment on she was obsessed with talking to Granddad." Pamela wiped at her cheeks, her nose again. "She tried all of them, and I went with her to most visits, though I was busy, I had school. And guilt." She let out a small, humorless laugh. "I had no idea by letting her go alone I was leaving her open to predators."

"She found Sadie." The only truth that made sense.

"She was Prairie Wind then," Pamela spit out. "Claimed to be Native American, all feathers and dreamcatchers and fake totems. Made me sick. But, by the time I realized she was a fraud, Gramma was in so deep she'd given the woman most of the money she and Granddad had managed to save. Her only nest egg, gone to that horrible, horrible woman."

I held still, let her go on without prompting.

"She bilked my grandmother out of everything she had, left her with her tiny pension and skipped town. Gramma was horrified when she realized, embarrassed. She died a month later, of a broken heart, in a crappy little nursing home because I was a kid and didn't have the money to help her."

Oh, Pamela. Sounded like motive for murder.

Crap.

"I spent years tracking her down." Yikes, I had to stop her right there, I needed her to get a lawyer or something because I couldn't sit here and listen to this. Not in good conscience. "Used my job to hunt her." She whipped her head around and glared at me. "I'm not asking you to listen to keep your mouth shut, okay? I promise. You can tell Crew everything when I'm done. I'd never ask that of you, Fee."

I nodded. "Okay. Keep going." Heart heavy, I waited for my friend to tell me she was guilty and hated myself for doing it.

"I was obsessed, I admit it," Pamela said, sitting back, petting Petunia, as if telling me she was planning to confess took her anxiety away. She seemed relaxed suddenly, at peace with her story. "It took nine years and a lot of money, but I finally found her." This time when she laughed it was kind of dazed, soft and sorrowful. "I cornered her outside the back of her shop. She'd seen me coming and tried to sneak away. I told myself I was doing this for the story, to protect the public, for the greater good. But the second I saw her, the instant I was close enough, I punched that woman in the face as hard as I could."

"The assault charge," I said.

"She had the nerve to call the police." Pamela seemed oddly impressed by that. "I'll tell you, it was an awakening. I broke off my pursuit, let her go, told them what I knew. I got community service and served it then went back to work for a decade. Poured myself into the job until I couldn't take being alone anymore and came home." I knew what alone felt like, a quiver of further sympathy stirring the need to cry. "To Reading. To Aundrea. And forgot about the woman who hurt my grandmother."

Now for the hard part. "Until Sadie showed up. Prairie Flower. Whoever."

Pamela nodded. "I knew who she was the second I saw her, but I don't think she recognized me. The old compulsion came back, to track her, to find a way to turn her over to Crew. I wanted to do it right this time, Fee." So much intensity in her face, in her entire body. "I wanted her to go to jail for what she was doing."

"Why didn't you?" Surely there was enough evidence to be had.

"I had to be careful this time. I started gathering information, her aliases. I ended up taking everything to him just last week." She tensed before blowing air through her thin lips. "All the good it did me."

"He didn't act?" Okay, now I was pissed. Because this was his fault, then. Sadie's death was on him, not me.

"He said he had his own digging to do." She shrugged then, and a sad smile twisted her mouth, tugged at the lines around her eyes. "I should have let it go."

I knew that particular tune. Could sing the entire song all by myself, even be my own backup band. "You didn't."

"I didn't." Pamela leaned ahead, elbows on her knees, Petunia protesting her lost attentions. "I went to the séance to confront her. To get firsthand knowledge of her little fraud and then write a story exposing her." She seemed to struggle with her thoughts a moment. "Aundrea knew nothing. I kept it from her. Partly because I was embarrassed by my failure and partly because this was my burden. It had nothing to do with her." Aundrea said as much, though I wondered at Pamela's refusal to accept help. I was pretty sure her partner would have loved to carry some of the weight bowing my friend's shoulders. Not for me to decide, though. "I know it was stupid. I'd done what I could already. Publishing a story like that would have led to slander charges. Still, I couldn't let it go."

"So you killed her." Now what was I going to do? Call Crew? Tell Dad? This was a disaster.

Pamela spun on me, shock on her face. "No!"

Hang on. What? "You didn't come here to confess?"

She spluttered, turned red, tried to rise, to leave. I jerked her back down beside me, heart pounding and faced her with the kind of sternness I knew would make Mom proud.

"Pamela," I said, slowly and with care, "you told me you were in trouble. You came to my door wanting to confess something. Even told me to tell Crew everything. So what did you think I'd assume?"

She gaped a moment then swallowed hard. "I'm sorry. No, Fee. I didn't kill her." She sagged against me, Petunia between us getting the brunt of it but uncomplaining. "But I didn't tell Crew about my history with her. I know that's going to make me look bad."

"Looking bad we can handle," I said. "Murder, not so much."

She laughed, shaky and soft. "I'm an idiot."

"It's going around," I said. "You're in excellent

company."

She smiled at me then, like telling me about it lifted her lingering past from her shoulders. "Now what do I do?"

"Go talk to Crew," I said. "Tell him why you gathered the information in the first place. And make sure you take a lawyer with you."

She clamped her fingers together in front of her. "I will," she said. "I've just been so…" Another deep sigh, from the depths of her. "I knew this would make me look like a suspect and I didn't know how to talk to him. But you're right, I'm being ridiculous."

"Let me ask you something," I said, intuition firing, because there was more than one source of information in this town and I was looking right at one of the best. "Before you run off and do the right thing and give Crew Turner an aneurism for withholding information." She flashed a quick smile. Clearly I wasn't the only one who bore the brunt of his temper, then. Good to know.

"Anything," she said.

She might regret that offer. "What do you know about Sadie's connection to Oliver Watters?"

CHAPTER TWENTY-FIVE

PAMELA SEEMED STARTLED BY my question. "I didn't know they had one."

Okay, so not as helpful as I'd hoped. "What about Manuel Cortez?" And now I was all over the place with my questions, her confusion apparent.

"What are you looking for, Fee?" She switched back into newspaper mode, at least, her confession time over with and the inquisitive mind returned. Hmmm. Maybe I should have gone into investigative journalism rather than police work. Shook that off as I answered with the information Dad and I dug up.

Pamela's growing frown about my suggestion Sadie's death might have been connected to the

Cortez boy only told me she wasn't open to such thinking just yet.

"Trust me," she said, voice vibrating with anger, "this is all about Sadie. She earned that death, Fee, as sad as it is for me to admit. Someone had a bone to pick, likely connected to money she defrauded them, and they killed her for it."

I wasn't about to take her word for it, only because she had her own agenda still. "I shouldn't even be asking," I said then. "I really need to mind my own business." Part of me hated hearing those words, a mimic of the ones that I'd been hearing from others since Pete died. And part of me, I admit, was looking for validation.

Pamela gave it to me, in spades. Her eyes twinkled suddenly, a grin breaking over her face. "You would have made a great reporter, Fee." There was that idea again. Finding a route to validate my need to snoop, one way or another. But I had a business to run. Still, the speculation that crossed her face, the intake of breath held a huge, silent question I knew she was on the cusp of asking.

I didn't have an answer. Instead, I cut her off with a grin of my own.

"So, mind filling me in on the super secret project

Mom's cooking up for you and Aundrea?"

I meant that to be a casual and happy deflect. After all, Mom had been beaming over it, so surely it was a good thing, some kind of joyful occasion—I had my suspicions. Instead, Pamela deflated all over again, looking away, shaking her head.

"I should go," she said, standing abruptly. "Face the music with Crew."

I joined her, Petunia hopping down with a solid thud and a faint groan. "He'll understand. He knows you, Pamela."

She didn't leave immediately despite her words, staring at me a long moment before nodding. "You're right," she said, as if she'd been having a conversation with herself, or me, or who knew, in her head all that time. "I'm being closed minded about Sadie." I didn't comment, let her go on. "I do have one thing I uncovered when I did a quick check on the Cortez's, connected to the mother." She frowned over the details. "She was questioned in a disappearance about twenty years ago. One of her advisors for her masters." A soft tsk as if she judged herself for her lack of memory. "I have his name written down somewhere."

"Nothing came of it?" Pamela was killing me,

dragging me back into the mess like this. I could hug her for it, truthfully. I did have allies, though she was a snoop herself so maybe she didn't count.

"No," she said. "And the advisor was never found, foul play never proved. The man just vanished." Pamela's whole demeanor had changed, back to the old her I knew and respected. "I'll dig further. Talk to Oliver, find out what I can. And Alice." She smiled then. "And I'll get back to you with what I learn. If you'll consider something."

I knew what she was going to ask. Braced myself for it. "Okay."

"Write a column for me," she said. "I know you're busy, but Fee... just a column. Nothing huge. Will you think about it?"

Huh. Well, that wasn't the giant job offer I figured she'd be coming at me with. "About what?"

Pamela laughed. "You'll think of something."

I watched her go, heart beating a little too fast, mind whirling around the idea. I pushed myself to leave the sitting room, to get back to work, while I turned the offer over in my head. A column might be fun? Though, honestly, who would give two shakes about what I had to say? Still, if Pamela thought it might be worthwhile...

Food for thought.

With breakfast well under way and a few hours to kill before the new guests checked in at 1PM, I left Mom humming and Dad puttering to slip off to the hospital to check in on Betty. It was a quiet fifteen minute drive to Falls Station, enough time I actually found myself framing a Pulitzer Prize and hanging it on my wall, grinning at how silly I was being. Still, it kept me in a good mood the whole way, this possibility of doing something fun and different, so I was smiling when I walked into Betty's private room and found the sisters playing cards over the bandages around her knee.

A soap opera played out its tragic extravaganza in the background as they greeted me with smiles of their own. I hugged Mary, then Betty, before settling next to them both with my purse in my lap. From the tally sheet Mary was hoarding she was beating her sister badly, but I figured the pain meds would be a good excuse for losing at cards.

At least both seemed happy and relaxed and I wondered how much longer they'd be staying on at Petunia's despite their initial fears I'd be firing them when I first took over.

"Your mother called and stopped in twice," Mary

said, flipping a card onto the small hospital table with glee, almost upsetting Betty's Jell-O cup. Her normally silent sister grunted, frowning, before responding with a card of her own. They didn't seem to be playing a game I knew, so I stayed out of it.

Leave it to Mom to be so attentive, while I was just getting around to a check-in. Hello, guilt, my old friend. "She's keeping things tidy for you," I said, smiling at Betty. "She and Dad are a huge help, so don't worry about a thing."

They exchanged a look and I knew, the pit of my stomach tightening. They were going to leave me. I did my best not to cry, blinking and smiling and swallowing the lump in my throat. Instead of telling me they were retiring, Mary made small talk while Betty sampled her green cup of goo and continued to lose at cards.

Mary suddenly gasped, turning toward me, scattering the stack of cards on the table. Her wide eyes and open mouth made me start, too, until one of her wrinkled hands caught my wrist, clamping on there like she never planned to let go. "Another murder," she said. "Oh, Fee. I meant to say how sorry I was."

I shook my head, relaxing again. "I'm getting

used to it."

They both snorted amusement at that. "Are you staying out of trouble?" Mary's eyes sparkled with humor.

Yeah. Best not to go there.

"How's the knee?" I waited for Betty to answer, knowing better.

"She's been walking on it already," Mary said, no shocker there. I always wondered why Betty didn't talk, assuming she might be mute. But I'd overheard her mutter a curse or two in the course of our time together, so I knew that wasn't the case. Still, the sisters seemed happy with their arrangement and it certainly didn't bother me, as long as I got an answer of some kind.

"Good to know," I said. "Will they have to do the other one?"

Betty shook her head and Mary sighed. "We'll see."

They shared a mutual glare that made me grin.

I had a thought. "Did you two know Sadie, by any chance? When she lived in Reading?"

They both nodded in tandem, matching gray curls bobbing.

"We went to school together," Mary said, going

back to her cards while Betty tossed hers on the table, snatching for her sisters, shuffling the deck.

Huh. "Any idea what her connection was with Oliver Watters?" It was asked casually. I wasn't expecting much, to be honest. And got a shock when Mary hesitated, then answered.

"Her real name was Mildred, but everyone called her Sadie," she said. "And Oliver was in love with her."

CHAPTER TWENTY-SIX

I GAPED AT HER while she went on, blushing a little, meeting my eyes with her own full of guilt.

"I hate to speak ill of the dead," she said. Betty smacked the back of her hand and rolled her eyes and Mary shrugged, nodded. "The girl was born a flimflam artist. Got it from her grandmother, the first Sadie Hatch. No chance, that child, not one with her mother run off and leaving her to that reprobate to raise her."

Betty was nodding enthusiastically, dealing cards to her sister and then herself. I thought for a moment she actually might speak up, but Mary was already talking again.

"You couldn't trust her, not with a secret, not with a toy, not with a beau." She sighed then, staring at her hand like she didn't see the cards. Betty twitched at the mention of a boyfriend, as if her sister jabbed her personally instead of just speaking out loud. Her scowl deepened, eyes narrowing to tight lines. "I don't think it was her fault, Fee. Just the way she was raised. Broken, like."

Betty snorted like she disagreed, thumping cards down with more enthusiasm than was necessary. Utterly fascinating and horrible at the same time. "And Oliver?"

"He didn't see her bad side, refused to, not for a long time." Mary set her cards aside and sat back, crossing her arms over her ample chest, the sunlight from the tall window hitting her at an angle, making her pale eyes almost transparent, gray hair glowing faintly. Like some kind of rough around the edges fairy godmother sitting for a second to take a load off. "He loved her from when we were small, even before her mom left her with her grandma. Maybe he knew her before she turned bad to the bone, but I think she was born that way on account of who her family was."

Betty's grim expression turned sad, her own cards

still in her hands but not looking at them, staring at her sister as if to silence her if she could with her own lack of speaking. Not that it worked.

"We had the odd run-in, I'll admit it." Mary nodded abruptly to Betty whose lips now pursed into a narrow, tense slash in her sorrowful face. "She learned not to mess with us, right, Betts?"

Betty's whole expression shifted to fury, eyes meeting mine. All the answer I needed.

"Why did she leave town?" I almost didn't want to speak, enraptured by the story.

"There were rumors," Mary said, "no one knew for sure. But something to do with a pregnancy and one of the Pattersons." Ah. So Sadie's child who became who? Denver's dad since he used her last name? "Nothing proved, of course. I heard Sadie's grandma tried to blackmail the family. The old lady died about a year after the girl left town, heart attack. Though it was suggested she had help."

Okay, that was another coincidence in a chain of them I wasn't buying anymore. "The Pattersons made sure there wasn't an investigation, I take it?"

Mary and Betty shrugged in unison, both looking at me without speaking. Said volumes with their expressions instead.

As interesting as this history lesson was, it was making my head spin. Maybe Pamela was right and this was about Sadie, but not client based after all. Could it instead be about her coming home and maybe stirring up old trouble that the Patterson family wanted long buried? That meant Pamela wasn't a suspect, after all. No, that opened the door to Aundrea.

No, no way. She didn't like her family, didn't get along with them. So the likelihood Aundrea had anything to do with Sadie's death was pretty ridiculous. Still, there were enough Pattersons left with enough influence in their grasp it was very possible they'd not only done away with her grandmother but come after Sadie, too. Leaving Manuel Cortez's death unconnected and a particularly irritating red herring.

Definitely food for thought.

"Sadie left, and took all of Oliver's money with her." Mary sounded sad at last. "The money he'd told everyone who'd listen he'd set aside to buy them a house of their own. A ring. To get married with. Then she got pregnant by a Patterson, broke Oliver's heart and abandoned him."

Betty looked down abruptly, lower lip quivering,

while my mind stuttered over the history unfolding in my lap. Wow. That was definitely motive, too, if ever I heard it. So the Pattersons had reason, if Sadie was back to blackmail them. Goodness knew they'd done some despicable things to protect their name, Aundrea's marital misery a case in point. Would murder be a step too far? And then there was Oliver. If it had been the old historian, why did he wait this long, a year after her return, to do the deed?

"He turned so bitter." Mary leaned forward again, lifted her cards, sorted them as if looking for something to occupy herself while she continued to relive the past. "He's held a grudge all these years." She glanced at Betty ever so quickly, looked away again, while her sister continued to scowl down at her folded hands like they offended her.

I had a heartbreaking revelation, a moment of clarity, as the two sisters lingered in the dusty realm of ancient history. About possibility and the death of it. About a young woman who cared about a young man who couldn't see past the girl who was wrong for him to the one who loved him. Compassion hit me for Betty and her silence.

Of course, I had no idea if it was just my imagination running off with me. Likely. I was prone to it, after all. Yet, there was this sorrowful weight to the silence that followed, an old hurt that held Betty's tongue and made Mary sag in her chair.

"I'm sorry," I said. Neither acknowledged what I said. "Do you think he would have still hated her enough to kill her?"

Mary didn't answer, but Betty did, if not with words. She looked up swiftly, met my eyes, her jaw tight and a tiny, quick nod answering. Which told me she just might hold enough animosity of her own to do the deed. Except, of course, she'd been here in the hospital, her sister at her side. So I could check the Jones's off my list of suspects. I really was a horrible, horrible person.

"I do know one thing," Mary said. "That there's a healthy dose of doubt in my mind now about who actually got that girl pregnant." Oh, really? Betty threw her cards down in a huff, turning away to stare at the TV like what Mary was about to say hurt her deeply. "You can't deny it, Betts," Mary said, softer this time. She turned to me then, more sorrow in her face. "That grandson of hers? Ran into him at the bakery a week or so before Betty's surgery. I'd swear if I didn't know better, Fiona, he was Oliver all over again."

I gasped softly, startled by my own reaction. "You think he was the baby's father? That she lied to blackmail the Pattersons?" Checking them off my list of suspects? Surely a DNA test would be less risky than committing murder.

"Or her grandmother made her lie." Mary bobbed one last nod. "All I know is Denver looks just like Oliver did when he was that age. So you tell me."

"When did Denver come to live with Sadie?" I tensed then, pulse picking up tempo.

"About two weeks ago, I think? Not even." Mary tried to get confirmation from Betty but her sister refused to turn her head, to look away from her glare at the television across the room. Mary sighed at her but didn't make an issue about it. "At least that was the first time I saw him."

Denver had left MIT to come to Reading, but why? To sell his invention? Maybe he didn't think he needed school anymore. Or, more likely, to do as he'd said, to take the system away from his grandmother.

"Do you think Oliver would have made that connection?" Even more motive, as far as I was concerned. To discover the woman you loved not only shattered your trust and your heart but stole from you then lied to you, took your child away and you found out only decades later that she'd denied you access to your own flesh and blood? The timing would explain it, wouldn't it?

I had to talk to Crew. If he was talking to me at all.

Quick hugs all around, Betty still stiff but at least willing to embrace me. I left them in their quiet unhappiness, though as I turned and looked back Mary had coaxed Betty into picking up her cards and they were resuming their game. There was so much I didn't know about the elderly women who shared my life. When and if they returned to Petunia's I was going to make it my mission to find out more, to ask them questions, to spend time with them.

Right, because we had tons of time these days. Well, I'd be making time.

I sat in my car with Crew's number staring at me, pondering calling him. Hit dial, even, then hung up before the call could go through. Instead of going right home, or even to the sheriff's office to speak to him directly, I instead stopped at the library. I knew better than to go to Crew with just a story, despite the compelling nature of it. If I had an image to compare to Denver, one of Oliver as a young man, it would go a long way to proving the sisters right.

Mr. Lightmews, the librarian, huffed a little at my eagerness, but he led me to the old school archives in his slow and methodical way, skinny body hunched over permanently from a lifetime of being in that position, I suppose. I thanked him as he left me, his eyebrows raised but a faint smile on his face.

It didn't take me long to dig up a photo and, I had to admit, Mary was dead on. The image of Oliver was such a close match to Denver there was no question in my mind who his grandfather really was.

But, did Oliver know it? Had he made the connection and was there the night of Sadie's murder to confront her or kill her? Neither of them made any indication of their past together, at least that I saw. Oliver had been grumpy and argumentative, but certainly didn't seem to take it as personally as I would have if it was me.

I needed to go to Crew now, with this. I hovered at the counter, waiting for Mr. Lightmews to finish photocopying the picture for me while I chewed my poor bottom lip into puffiness—good thing that look was in right now—and told myself over and over to just go to the sheriff's office.

So why then did I find myself instead, traitor feet uncontrollable and body unresisting, on my way to Oliver's antique shop? I stepped inside, breathing the old, musty smell again, eyes adjusting to the dimness. I'd never been here before, aside from my disastrous visit yesterday. I used to love wandering through places like this in New York, looking for hidden treasures. Not that I needed anything. Grandmother Iris's taste was amazing and I loved everything she'd used to decorate Petunia's. But there was an odd mix of relaxing excitement to perusing things from the past, items that had history and secrets they'd never divulge.

Made me wonder if Oliver knew anything about the music box and if he might be of help if I asked. That was, pending the reveal of his status as a murderer.

Right. Focus.

He emerged from the back, spotted me instantly, froze. That angry expression was on his face again as he charged toward me. Instead of arguing, I held out the photo in silence. He stopped again, stared at it, then up at me. Neither of us spoke, though he did finally reach out and take it. I nodded to him, hoping it was enough, and left.

Oliver's healing wasn't my responsibility. But if he was Denver's grandfather, he deserved to know about it. It was up to him to decide if he would let his bitterness win over the chance to finally let go of Sadie.

Mind you, if he already knew about Denver I'd just told him I was onto him. Which made me a target, didn't it? Yeah, I was an idiot sometimes. Time to tell Crew what I knew and hopefully put an end to this case.

I was on my way back to my car when my phone buzzed. A text from Dad flashed on the screen.

Info on Manuel, he sent.

So, instead of the smart thing, I did the nosy thing and went home to find out what Dad uncovered. Didn't feel guilty about it or anything.

Sure, Fee. If you say so.

CHAPTER TWENTY-SEVEN

DAD WAS WAITING FOR me at the door, and while not exactly excited enough to seem out of synch with the fact someone was murdered, he was a bit light in his step as he pulled me inside and guided me quickly into the sitting room to dish what he'd uncovered.

"My buddy in Boston said Manuel was cremated," he said, "by request of his parents." Not out of the ordinary per se, though it did seem rather suspicious to me considering there was still questions his mother asked about how he died. But how was this tied to Sadie? Or was it at all? I needed to tell Dad about Emelia's missing advisor, too. So many threads, one of them had to snap eventually. "The tox screen came back inconclusive, but Bob's doing some digging for me. Said the case file he looked at wasn't as thorough as it could have been." Dad seemed annoyed by that, though it surprised me his buddy was willing to admit it. Talking smack about a coworker wasn't really in the code, was it? "He's in a different precinct, said the boys that handled it are overloaded and agreed to let him look into it, so we'll see if he digs up anything further."

Either way, we'd hopefully be able to put Emelia's mind at ease that the case had new eyes.

I proceeded to tell Dad everything I'd uncovered, including Emelia's run-in after her mentor's disappearance. He let me hurry on until I ended with my encounter with Oliver, a little breathless to pour it all out at once. "What do you think?"

He grinned tightly before pulling me to my feet. "Let's go ask the expert."

At least I wasn't alone going to Crew's office, facing his flat expression or the scowl that evolved when we told him we needed to talk to him. Nice to have backup and my dad next to me when we sat down at Crew's desk—my father's old desk—and told him what we knew.

I was expecting more disappointment or the

inevitable shouting or even a brief and unhappy meeting ending in him kicking us out. Instead, Crew walked to the window and stared outside while Dad and I talked, filling in the bits and pieces we'd uncovered as the sheriff listened in silence. At least he didn't look tense. If anything, he seemed relaxed, hands in his back pockets, shoulder against the casing, not looking at us but clearly paying attention as he nodded occasionally.

"So you like Emelia for this?" He startled me when he spoke up, after I'd finished with the last bit about Oliver and Denver and my guess about their relationship. I looked at Dad who nodded for me to answer, a faint smile on his lips.

"I don't know," I said. "Oliver seems to have a strong motive. Though if Emelia did find out Sadie was lying to her and came here for revenge… she was so distraught, it's possible her grief drove her to hurt the woman who deceived her."

"We can't discount the similarity of their deaths," Dad said in his rumbling baritone, crossing one ankle over the opposite knee, tapping his chin with his finger, elbow propped on the armrest. "But it's possible it's just a coincidence and that Sadie's death is totally unrelated. It could be Manuel is connected to the disappearance of her advisor instead and Sadie is a casualty of another killer." Great, because we needed more murderers hanging around Reading. He looked up at Crew who hadn't turned back to us yet. "Any news on the tox panel?"

The sheriff finally did spin toward us, head down, dark hair shadowing his forehead, stubble thick on his cheeks. There was a weariness about him that bothered me and I wondered how well he was handling this job, the pressure of taking on this county. Though, Dad managed it. Surely Crew could, too. I suppressed the guilty feeling the tiredness came not from his job but from my interference.

"Not yet," Crew said, crossing to sit behind his desk, leaning back, eyes locked on the surface. "I should have something later today. Doc said they just need to identify the compound that was used, but they're backlogged." He fell quiet then, the room growing oppressive with each passing second, soft ticking of the clock on the wood paneled wall getting louder and louder, at least to me. "I wasn't aware Emelia Cortez had anything in her past that raised red flags." He didn't seem overly upset by that fact, but I wouldn't want to be Robert later. So much for the tiny scrap of respect I'd raised for my cousin's work. Apparently he sucked at being a cop. Made me more than a little giddy because I was petty like that.

"So, poison," I said, interrupting the awkward silence and my own need to giggle over Robert's failings. "That's typically a woman's weapon." I hated to typecast, but it was true.

"Back to Emelia." Crew finally looked up, but he met Dad's eyes instead of mine. "Unless there's a more viable suspect neither of you has focused on." Emotionless, that delivery, too flat for my liking.

"Meaning?" Dad tilted his head, tension around his eyes the only indication he wasn't impressed with Crew's attitude or being challenged for missing something.

Crew's gaze never left dad as my curiosity fired off while he spoke. "What about Alice Moore?"

She hadn't even crossed my radar as a possible suspect. "What about her?" I glanced at Dad who frowned, shook his head. "She's a blogger, a debunker." Wait, I'd noticed in my research she'd been pretty focused on Sadie, right? And failed to uncover why.

"Sadie has fled two locations because of Alice's interference," Crew said, sitting forward, hand falling on a closed file in front of him. "That I've found so far."

"Which means, if anything, Sadie should have had it out for Alice," I said, "not the other way around." Defensive much?

Crew didn't comment, except to go on. "Alice did nothing to turn Sadie in. Just showed up, asked questions, made people pay attention. For someone actively trying to shut her down, she did surprisingly little to get her arrested."

I couldn't think of an argument to that, though it raised an obvious question. "Why?"

He finally met my eyes, his empty and flat. "Because, Fee," he said, an edge coming to his tone at last, like this was the last thing he wanted to be doing. As if breaking down his case to the pair of us hurt him so much he could barely stand it. Didn't stop him from finishing his explanation. "Alice used to work for Sadie." Bomb dropped. Whoa. "Before the old lady set her up to take the fall and the girl ended up in jail for fraud."

CHAPTER TWENTY-EIGHT

I MUST HAVE LOOKED ridiculous sitting there with my mouth open and my forehead scrunched as I processed what he said. I'd trusted Alice, believed in her. No way I'd misread her or her need for answers. Um-hum, all my history of having great instincts about people argued otherwise while a jolt of hurt she might have been lying to me cut deeper than it should have.

Okay, time to be honest with myself. Was I defending her because I liked her, or because I thought she was innocent despite evidence that suggested the contrary? Evidence I myself discovered? It was clear Alice targeted Sadie, and now I knew why.

But was she working with Sadie still? Or, had she been following the woman around as some kind of fraud of her own devising? Setting herself up as this big debunker to get views on her blog? Could all of her success be tied to a lie set up and perpetuated by the old woman, using Alice's blog influence in some convoluted plan the two con artists used to bilk customers?

No. I couldn't believe that. And yet, there was zero doubt I'd been a terrible judge of character in the past, hadn't I? Hardly unbelievable someone could pull one over on me.

Dad, at least, wasn't frozen by hurt and surprise. "How long ago?"

"Four years." Crew tapped the file again, hesitated briefly, shrugged like he'd decided it wasn't in his best interest to fight any longer. I didn't like the defeat on his face as he went on, though it faded as he spoke. "She ran a con with Sadie in Des Moines, though she professed her innocence at the time. Still, her alleged partner disappeared and left Alice holding the incriminating evidence—namely the blackmail payment she picked up during a sting operation."

Wow. Alice couldn't have been more than

eighteen at the time, still only in her early twenties. How horrible for her. Undeniably motive. As long as she wasn't still working with Sadie. Though, if the old woman had gotten me arrested for a crime I didn't knowingly commit I'd have hunted her down. Worse if I'd known about it and was of a more murderous and criminal bent to begin with.

Wasn't looking good for my new friend.

"She pled down, got a short stint in county for first offense and was released early for good behavior." Crew pushed the file toward Dad who helped himself while I ignored it, focusing on the sheriff as he went on. "Ended up with a record, though. Sounds like she struggled a bit before she started that blog of hers. From her financials, she's been funding herself off the proceeds." He shrugged, looked puzzled. "I guess there's a big market for paranormal investigations online. She has enough reported advertising income to keep her comfortable."

"But nothing to indicate she was still working with Sadie." Please, at least he could confirm that.

Crew opened his hands wide, shaking his head. The moment his frown returned, I knew he was done leaving backgrounds up to anyone else ever again, let alone Robert. "I'm still digging." I just bet he was.

Dad skimmed the file before snapping it shut and returning it to Crew's desk. "So, two options for Alice, then. Either she killed her partner for an undisclosed reason or she murdered Sadie in revenge for sending her to prison."

"I don't buy it." Okay, so I was defending my friend without any kind of backup. But I really didn't believe it. "Maybe—maybe—if they were still working together, there might have been a reason we haven't seen yet. But if Alice was going to kill Sadie, it sounds like she had lots of chances. According to her blog she tracked the woman all over the country. She had tons of opportunity that didn't involve witnesses and didn't act."

"Maybe the timing was just off or there could have been a trigger we still don't know about." Crew's level tone was starting to get on my nerves.

Fine. We'd just see about that. As soon as I got home and cornered Alice. No mincing around the past she shared with the victim. Time to ask her some tough questions.

"Did Pamela talk to you?" At least I knew *she* was innocent.

Crew arched his eyebrows at me, but that was the

only change in his expression. "She told me the rest of the story," he said. "She's on the radar, Fee." Then held up both hands as Dad and I tried to talk at the same time. "Okay, okay. Fine, stop, please. The last thing I need is a Fleming tag team right now." I was hoping for a bit of a smile, but his expression didn't change. "There are enough victims out there of Sadie Hatch's fraud that we may be missing someone in the pool of suspects." He sighed finally, rubbed his forehead with one hand as if he tried to massage away a headache.

"Crew." Dad paused like he knew what he was going to say wasn't going to go over very well. "I know we're interfering." The sheriff snorted, looked up, finally cracked a smile.

"You do, do you, John?" He glanced at me, then back to Dad. "Wow. I doubted, you know. But here you're proving to me you really are a detective."

Dad grinned despite Crew's tone. His sarcasm might have made me feel uncomfortable, but my father wasn't letting it get to him. At least, he didn't seem to take it personally, smile fading into concern. "We're not making your life any easier. I hear Olivia is breathing down your neck."

Crew stiffened, face grim then flattening out

again. "I can handle her and the council, thanks." He cleared his throat. "You've been more than helpful in that area already."

Which meant we'd been adding to his difficulties from a number of sides I wasn't aware of. Whoops.

"I know you're up for the job," Dad said, not trying to soothe his successor, but using that kind of tone that felt so man-to-man the testosterone levels in the room jumped about 1000%. "That's not in question." Crew seemed to relax a little at that. "What I'm saying is you have certain assistance at your disposal. And while neither of us are officially affiliated with this office, wasting energy arguing with that assistance instead of accepting the information uncovered might not be the best use of your time." The fact Dad just rolled me into the offer to help with him warmed my chilled heart just a little. Us, huh?

Crew didn't respond for a long moment. When my phone dinged, alerting me to a text message, I jumped, knowing I winced, though Crew used the interruption to break his own silence. "I can't authorize or approve of the two of you running off and interfering with police business, John. Bad enough I've been as open with you as I have been, both today and in the past." His jaw clenched briefly. "And don't think I'm not aware of the fact a computer outside our system accessed police files using the new password."

Oops. Caught red handed. Dad just shrugged.

"Do you want our help or not?" There it was, out on the table, bare bones and blatant. Not that it was going to stop Dad, apparently, whatever Crew said, but I guess he wanted to know where he stood. I already had an excellent idea, thanks to my conversation with the sheriff last night. Braced myself for the train wreck barreling toward us, hands clasping the arm rests of my chair on instinct.

That's why I was so surprised when Crew leaned forward, elbows on the desk, and faced off with my father, all anger gone, a faint trace of amusement in his eyes.

"Is this the moment, then?" He grinned. "You ready to be deputized for real, John Fleming?"

CHAPTER TWENTY-NINE

THE SECOND TIME SINCE I sat down I found my chin in my lap, looking back and forth between Crew and Dad like this was one of the melodramatic soaps Mary and Betty loved so much. Lost in the moment of their confrontation with my heart pounding, a huge question in my own mind fed by the delight Dad had been taking in investigating this case.

No way did Crew just offer to make Dad a cop again. No. Way. And yet, it seemed like that was exactly what the sheriff had done.

I thought Dad would laugh it off, to be honest. Snort over the idea, make a joke of it to ease the tension. Or tell Crew where to go with his stoic calmness firmly in place, that John Fleming didn't need no stinking deputization. Instead, face tight, anger apparent but unspoken, my father surged to his feet, throat working, cheeks growing redder and redder while his hands clenched into fists at his sides. Wait, what was happening? He acted like they'd had this conversation before, as if he'd already answered in the past, that this was the kind of challenge Crew knew could set my father off.

Had this come up and I didn't know? Sure seemed that way.

Before I could splutter out a question, my shock at their faceoff tying my tongue into a knot, Dad spun and stormed out of the office, slamming the door behind him. Leaving me alone with Crew whose mildly surprised expression told me he wasn't expecting Dad to react like that, either.

Silence held for a long moment, to the sound of stomping through the thin walls, the angry jangle of the bells as Dad left, the thud as he forced the glass door closed despite the soft hinges that prevented slamming. Close enough. Another few seconds ticked by before Crew sighed, finally meeting my eyes, letting me see his openness a moment until he purposely shut down again.

"What about you, Fee?" His voice was soft, but there was nothing gentle about his tone, no amusement this time like he'd held for Dad. "You plan to take a badge? Train on the job, even. That can be arranged, if it suits you. Olivia would be delighted, the whole council, as a matter of fact, to have a Fleming back on the force." His nostrils flared while I processed his words and came up with an uncomfortable truth. Is that what this was about? The council and mayor had been pressuring Crew, not to solve the crime, but to include me and Dad in the investigation? That had to rankle. Personally, I wasn't sure he should have felt so insulted, though. Dad was, at least, great at the job. I guess including me wasn't exactly encouraging, though, was it? Nor did it give the impression the town had much faith in their sheriff.

At least now I knew why he was so upset. Empathy woke, promises I likely wouldn't keep on my lips, when Crew went ahead and finished his thought and guaranteed the two of us would end this talk in anger.

"I'm sure Robert would be overjoyed to mentor you, if that's what you really want."

Choke. Splutter. Growl. Like *hell*. "You know

that's never going to happen," I said, chest tight with more words I wanted to spit in his face. He was just being a jerk at this point.

"Then," Crew leaned closer, "get out of my office and my business and go back to Petunia's, Fee. Because if you're not going to step up, you're making my job harder." I opened my mouth to respond but he wasn't done. "You just don't get it." His head lowered a moment, hands clenching in front of him. "You don't understand at all and it's driving me crazy."

But I did, or thought I did. Gave him the benefit of the doubt despite my lingering anger. "Tell me." I didn't want to hear what he had to say, braced for the hurt that was coming, stomach heaving, all the blood rushing from my face. I needed to know.

When he looked up again and his blue eyes caught mine it wasn't fury or judgment or even frustration there. Just his own pain. Not at all what I'd prepared for. So I was in no kind of condition to respond when he spoke again.

"Just go, please." He sat back, half turned away from me. "I have work to do."

I stumbled to my feet, retreated without a word, paused at the door as my breath came back, as my heart started beating a normal rhythm again, all anger gone in the face of the pain I caused him. "I know I'm butting my nose in where I'm not wanted, and sometimes I get into more trouble than I'm worth. But I can't help it. I'm sorry, I really can't. You were right. I try so hard, but when I tell myself I'm not going to interfere it just all falls apart and I stumble into something that makes me ask questions."

Crew didn't respond, just sat there.

Instead of trying again, the need to explain myself despite the fact he'd already told me last night he understood my motivation making me sick to my stomach, I left. At least I didn't feel the need to slam his door.

Fortunately only Toby was in the office, so I didn't have to face Jill's sympathy or Robert's arrogant smarminess. I managed a bit of a smile for the sad receptionist and headed home.

It didn't take me long to accept that I'd pretty much burned my last bridge with Crew, that any possible chance of a relationship with him ended back there in his office. It sucked, because like my innate curiosity, there was something about him that made it so hard to just walk away. Time to find a way, though. In all honesty, did I really want to date someone who saw me as a troublemaking snoop who just caused him problems and made him feel like the people who hired him didn't trust him to do his job without help?

I really had terrible taste in men.

I was two blocks from home, head down, thoughts spinning, when I remembered my phone, the text message. Was reaching for it and almost didn't notice when the black car pulled up next to me, back passenger window winding down. It wasn't until someone whistled I stopped in my tracks and peeked inside, seeing, to my shock, Malcolm Murray on the far side of the back bench seat, smiling at me.

"Fiona," he called out my name in that amazing accent of his, making it sound exotic. "Care for a drive, dearie?"

One of his big bullies got out of the front passenger side and opened the door for me, waiting with expectation. So the offer wasn't a request, then.

"Um, I'm just around the corner," I said. "And you're heading the wrong way."

Malcolm shrugged, winked. "Humor me."

This was a terrible idea. Since I was the queen of terrible ideas, I found myself, as always, controlled by compulsion and questions, crossing the distance and sliding in beside him, the door closing firmly on me and triggering a brief flash of dread.

When exactly had I lost my freaking mind again?

CHAPTER THIRTY

MALCOLM LEANED FORWARD, TAPPING his driver on the shoulder before sinking back into the soft leather of the seat. I had to admit it was luxuriously comfortable, though I found it hard to settle in as we pulled away from the side of the road and into traffic. Heading for the other side of town at a leisurely pace. My overactive imagination began to whisper to me that no one I loved might ever see me again, that Malcolm had lured me into a false sense of security and now was taking me to die in some remote location where wild animals would dig up my body and eat me and Mom and Dad would never know what happened—

"Fiona." I started, meeting my host's eyes. His were full of laughter, one hand patting my knee. "Relax. It's just a drive."

So he said. I swallowed, tried to act casual and failed utterly. "What is it between you and my father?" Way to gush out a question that could get you killed, Fleming. Nice job. Classy.

Malcolm didn't seem surprised, though. "Exactly the reason I wanted to have this little conversation, lassie," he said. "In private. Since your da is so intent on keeping us apart." He seemed equally amused and irritated by that.

"I noticed," I said.

He snorted a chuckle. "You're a lot like him, more than you know." His eyes watched me a long moment, smile almost sad. "He named you well." Why did that come out so full of sorrow?

Malcolm cleared his throat at last, reaching into his breast pocket, pulling out a card. He held it in his hand as he spoke, head down, the sunlight catching the silver of his close-cropped hair, the hint of it stubbled over his cheek.

"There was a time your da and I had a different relationship than we do now," Malcolm said. I almost had to strain to hear him, leaning closer as he went on. "Things didn't start out for the best, Fiona. Nor did they end up the way I thought they would. But life goes on, doesn't it? We adapt, do our best to make the most of the cards we've been dealt. No matter what the burden we carry because of the actions we've taken. Or the hurt we've caused that haunts us."

Wow, he had enigmatic down to an art form. "That tells me so much," I said, temper shaking me out of my fear, "and so very little at the same time."

He laughed again, eyes crinkling in the corners in genuine good humor. "Forgive me, it's my nature to cling to the mystery. I've always loved it. I think we share it, maybe." He grinned then, pointed at me with the card in his hand but didn't give it over just yet. I made out a name hand written on one side, partially covered by his thumb. "You'll do well to do your own investigating," he said then. "And, when you do, we'll talk again, shall we?"

He finally handed me the card and I took it with a thrill of nervousness and more than a little anxiety. Malcolm didn't release it right away, staring into my eyes for a moment, the kindest and gentlest expression on his face as his free hand lifted tentatively. For a second I thought he was going to touch me, my hair, but instead he let both hands fall, the card now in my possession at the same instant the car came to a halt and his bully in the front seat got out.

"I'll be looking forward to our next meeting," Malcolm said, the rush of cool air washing in through the open door beside me making me shiver. "Have a nice day, Fiona Fleming."

I found myself breathlessly watching him drive away, standing on the sidewalk outside Petunia's with the card clutched in my hand a long time before I had the courage to look down and read it.

His handwriting, I suppose, blocky and dark, like he used excessive force to ink the lines. A name, that was all. Siobhan Doyle. No number, no email, nothing. Just that name. Why did it feel like more than enough?

I tucked it into my coat, heart racing all over again. I'd go inside right now and search her name and find out what this was all about. Just as soon as I caught my breath.

Jared held the door for me as I entered the foyer and I found myself smiling with the kind of startled openness that came from walking from one shock to another. Until I remembered he'd wanted to talk to me.

"I'm glad you're here," he said. "Do you have a minute?"

Of course. Because I wasn't just planning to dig into my father's past and maybe uncover something that should remain buried. Why did it feel like nodding to Jared was running away from the truth I said I was looking for?

He led me outside, oddly, down the sidewalk, but not far. Just one door down, as a matter of fact. To the one place I never hoped to set foot again. As I stared at Peggy Munroe's front door, Jared spoke in a rushed avalanche of words like he expected me to turn tail and run away before he could finish.

Smart guy. I almost did.

"It's just sitting here and I need to do something with it. It's so close to you and you're busy, Fee, I know how busy you are." He was walking, tugging me along with him, still talking. Alicia stood on the front porch, holding the door open, smiling. As if he was a gameshow host and she his lovely blonde assistant in her short, black coat and tights, hand raised, gesturing at the entry.

Like they expected me to go inside.

Were they nuts? The last time I stood in that

foyer Peggy tried to kill me.

Except Jared had momentum and I was still reeling from my meeting with Malcolm with a sort of rubbery softness to my limbs that kept me from resisting.

That's how I found myself standing in the front entry with memories of Peggy and her gun and Petunia saving my life while I wrenched the weapon from the old woman's hand flashing in my head, Jared sketching out his idea.

Wait. What? "What?" I managed to speak at last, to process what he was saying. If I was going to be honest, the idea had briefly passed my own mind just a few months ago, but not seriously. There was no way this was going to happen.

"An annex," he smiled at me like he knew I was going to argue but figured it was worth a shot. "To Petunia's. Full reno, Fee, all updated and doubling your footprint." He gestured grandly before grinning as if such a physical motion was utterly ridiculous and he knew it. "It's the perfect move for this property. But we'll understand if you say no."

I stuttered a moment before shaking my head and taking a deep breath. "Again," I said. "Slowly this time. It's been a long day already and I'm a bit distracted. You want me to buy this place and turn it into an annex to my bed and breakfast and drive me insane in the process while I juggle what I already can barely handle with even more of the crazy I call a business?"

He nodded, Alicia beaming. Sad part to their reaction? I hadn't meant to be funny.

"Or," she said, prodding him as if he'd failed to sell their plan sufficiently, "we keep the deed but become silent partners in the enterprise if you're more comfortable with that."

There was nothing comfortable about this whole conversation, but I didn't say that out loud. Wasn't sure I had to, actually. Surely my expression spoke for itself?

They weren't backing down, though. Jared seemed to take my silence as an expected response. "I know I might not be the person you want to partner with," he said. Okay, that wasn't exactly what I'd been thinking, though clearly he had his own reservations that had nothing to do with how crazy the idea was in the first place. "I'm still struggling to fix my reputation, thanks to my father. That's why we'd be fine with a silent partnership. I don't need my name out there, if you'd rather keep it quiet."

Wow, just no. "Jared," I said, voice shaking a little, emotions finally getting the better of me, "there's no one I'd be prouder to work with. Don't doubt that for a second." He was carrying his own burdens I wasn't part of and being selfish about that in this moment wasn't serving either of us.

His smile returned, relief in his eyes. "Thanks, Fee. So, will you think about it?" He glanced at Alicia. "I wanted to offer it to you first. Give you the initial option." He looked up the steps, around the foyer. "It was in my father's name, Peggy's only real mistake when it came to her schemes. I guess she thought he'd outlive her. Instead, when he died, it came to me." I didn't know that, though I was aware he was in control of the property. I assumed it wouldn't transfer full ownership until she died—hopefully behind bars. "It's a beautiful old place that deserves better than it's had since Peggy went to prison. It's crying out to be developed."

Something about the way he said it made my blood run cold. "First option?"

He flinched, Alicia smacking him in the arm before she shrugged.

"You'll find out soon enough," she said, "and as your friends we wanted to tell you before you heard on the rumor mill."

Because they weren't the rumor mill. "Tell me what?"

"We need to act if this is going to be viable," she said. "There's a submission in front of the council to allow the construction of a small, intimate hotel complex at the edge of town."

Shouldn't have been a surprise, but kind of was. "Okay," I said. Exhaled. Not like there wasn't enough business to go around. Except they weren't done dropping bombs. From the expression on their faces, they knew I wasn't going to be happy about what came next.

Jared actually winced when he spoke, with good reason, driving a fist of shock into my gut that left me without air and words and even the means to react.

"No yelling," he said, only half joking. No promises. "The plan," he said, "has been tabled by Vivian French."

CHAPTER THIRTY-ONE

I WENT FROM HOLY, no way, what the hell to fireworks exploding in my head but I didn't get to let them out through my mouth in a running string of swear words or incoherent shrieks of hideously pathetic protests, because Jared hurried on.

"We don't want her submission to get accepted," he said. "And one way to block it is to develop this place as an annex."

"We already have approval," Alicia told me, holding tight to my elbow while I trembled my way past the initial shock of Vivian's plan to intrude on my business, the fact her hypocrisy wasn't lost on me making things worse. She'd been planning to get into my industry and here she was torturing my mother for what? To get back at me? Or for making a few cakes for Daisy's parties?

And then it hit me. This was what the whole poking and prodding situation had been about at the Halloween party. Vivian showed, on purpose, dressed like a witch—again, on purpose—to find out if I knew yet. Likely if Daisy hadn't saved me, would have filled me in then and there. Had been building up to the final, fatal blow so she could be the one to deliver the news.

Why then hadn't she said anything when I confronted her at the bakery? Didn't matter now. Or make me hate her any more, really. Just cemented my feelings for the backstabbing piece of trash.

I jerked myself out of my flash of insight into Vivian when Alicia's meaning hit me. Wait, what did she say? "You applied already?" Of course they had. I couldn't bring myself to think I'd be standing here with them if they'd planned to stab me in the back, too. It was pretty clear Reading needed more rooms to rent.

"We just wanted to be sure everything was in place before we brought it to you." Jared stepped away, turning to face me, hands in the pockets of his wool coat, face tired but a faint smile there. "Olivia jumped on the yes, and so did the town planner. We just need you to agree to it and we can move forward."

Again a flashback, Olivia at the party and at the sheriff's yesterday. Her suggestion/command I meet her at her office to talk. About this? Had to be. I'd purposely ignored her. Surprisingly she hadn't pursued me on the issue. Was that because of Jared and Alicia convincing her they wanted to tell me themselves?

"We should warn you." Alicia winced a bit, shrugged. "If you say no, you're probably going to get a visit from the mayor."

Little did they know I kind of already had. Though I was sure she'd be less suggestive and more commanding the third time around. Lovely. Just what I needed, a bullying session from our already stressed and overworked Olivia Walker. "Is she going to approve Vivian's hotel plan?"

"From what we know," Jared said, "if you agree to this, Olivia will kybosh the new complex. But." He shook his head, shrugged his wide shoulders. "It's only a matter of time, I think. As long as things stay as busy as they are. Reading is expanding at a pretty good clip."

"Though we both wonder how long that can last." Alicia's more practical side chose just then to show up.

Was she right? Maybe this was a terrible idea for other reasons. If tourism died off when Olivia lost the election—and my parents both seemed to think her exit was inevitable—would I be left with a giant debt and a huge new location no one would want to rent? The idea of losing Petunia's to bankruptcy wasn't exactly trust-inducing. "I never wanted this." I didn't. But to be honest, as I stood there and thought about it—shafting Vivian aside—the more I realized I liked the idea, risks or not. I'd inherited Petunia's debt-free, even gaining a small amount as an extra over and above full, outright ownership. Even not knowing what I was doing the first little while I'd done excellent business the last sixteen months and despite the threat of losing Olivia at the helm with her drive for tourism, surely her successor would follow in her footsteps? I had quite a lovely nest egg set aside thanks to how busy we'd been, enough, no doubt, for a down payment at the least, with a renovation fund to boot. "It does make sense." Wait, what did I just say? They both beamed at me and I exhaled, sagging a bit. "Give me a day or so to figure things out," I said at last, unable and unwilling to let myself make a snap decision while my head wasn't screwed on straight. "Okay?"

Alicia squealed like I'd said yes and hugged me, Jared's crooked grin answering her excitement.

I left them on the front walk, heading for Jared's truck, and went home alone, head spinning even more than it had been. Talk about an eventful morning. I was already in the kitchen at Petunia's before I realized I'd taken two steps, startled to find Amos there, making tea.

"I'm sorry," he said quickly, turning with a spoon in one hand and a little jar of honey, perky red label printed with gold in the other. "There was no one here and Emelia asked for tea."

"No problem." I managed to smile, to pretend I wasn't torn in three directions at once, shrugging off my jacket and discarding it on the back of a stool. "Can I help?" I glanced at the tray he'd made, the teapot, the cups. I'd have to buy all new everything for the annex. Not just new, but I had to think about branding, right? That was the word, wasn't it? Making everything look the same? Or, could I make the annex totally different, and keep them distinct from one another? Maybe turn it into a high end location?

"Miss Fleming?" Amos's dark eyes watched me with curiosity. "Are you all right?"

Whoops, daydreaming wasn't helping any. I smiled for real now, feeling a tiny ball of excitement in the pit of my stomach and wondering if I was far enough down the road to insanity I was actually going to say yes to Jared and Alicia.

"Just pondering some news," I said. "How is Emelia?"

He looked down at the tray, face grim. "I think she's coming out the other side at last," he said, though he didn't sound happy about it. "We're talking again. So, as horrible as the murder was, maybe this trip was a good idea after all." His hands twitched, the cups rattling, the jar of honey tipping sideways. I grasped for it, caught it before it toppled and righted it for him.

Frowned at the label. "This isn't ours?"

He shook his head, faint smile returning after momentary darkness. "Emelia's favorite brand," he said. "Special bees from Maine. She swears nothing tastes the same."

Huh. Maybe I should do an internet search for it

and stock it. If the annex was going to be more upper crust, things like special honey would be a detail I should pay attention to.

Jeeze, Fee. You're really going to do this, aren't you?

Amos left before I could say another word and I rolled my eyes at my own lack of attention. Poor man. At least it sounded like he and his wife were finally going to be able to move on from their loss.

That being said, could I move on, too? I leaned against the counter, staring into the garden through the kitchen windows, and across the fence at the house I'd mostly tried to avoid since the night Peggy Munroe pulled a gun on me. Could I erase the vague sense of horror I had for the place and make it my own?

I didn't want to think about the fact she was still alive, rotting in prison for murdering her grandnephew, for blackmail and assorted other crimes. Taking over her former home—a place she'd lived most of her adult life—just felt creepy.

What better way, though, to make use of her residence than to turn it into a happy stop for tourists? The more I thought about it, the more I liked the idea. It really was a stunning old place, much like Petunia's, with three stories towering inside a shade of tall maple trees. The garden was overrun, but that wouldn't take much to clean out. And the fence could finally come down. I hated it, such an eyesore. Something more elegant could replace it, maybe a cobbled walk or even a central fountain. The koi from the pond would love their own little meandering river, Fat Benny and his buddies flashing into my mind. With a lovely iron bridge spanning the winding flow…

Mom and Dad reappeared as the front door bell rang. 1PM and my guests. Right, then. Work it was.

I had little time to myself the rest of the day, the house full when I finally peeked into the kitchen to find it empty. Mom must have gone out for some groceries. Hadn't she mentioned she was low on some things? Wherever Dad had gone off to, I was sure he'd be back.

The phone rang, jerking me out of my trajectory for the coffee pot, needing a hit of caffeine. I ran to answer but hung up on the telemarketer who tried to sell me tickets for a cruise. I leaned against the wall, hands pressed to my heart, smiling to myself over how much fun the afternoon and early evening had been chatting with new guests, suggesting local dining spots, loving being their host and welcoming them to Reading. While my heart stretched and sighed and told me the direction I was leaning led me across the fence and into Peggy's yard.

I was nuts to consider it, already insanely busy. It was easy to think about Vivian, discard any kind of excuse saying yes was retaliation, though it would be satisfying to know she would be put off at least a little while. No, agreeing to the madcap scheme of the annex was all me wanting to do it because it would be fun and a challenge that maybe could erase my loneliness with activity and excitement.

Wouldn't it? The last few hours proved to me I truly loved what I was doing. So why the hell not?

I pushed away from the wall, turned to the phone hanging there, planning to call Jared immediately, stopped when I noticed the blinking red light that indicated messages. Right. I had this place to run in the meantime. If I was going to commit to growing my business, I had to be sure nothing fell to the wayside.

Ten minutes and six messages jotted later and I checked the final one, feeling satisfied and calm. Mom was the first, letting me know she was, indeed, at the grocery and would be back in an hour or so, that she had Dad and Petunia with her. The others were guests checking for bookings. But it was that last one that made me forget my future plans and focus on the here and now.

"Hey, John, Bobby here. Sorry to be late getting back to you, took me a while to dig out the M.E. file." Must be the friend of Dad's he was talking about, the detective in Boston. I hesitated, almost hit save, planning to listen with my father. But he'd given him this number, my number, so I guiltily took responsibility for the info and wrote it down as his message rattled on. "Turns out blood tests were done, but the whole thing was mishandled. There's a report here the samples got mixed up with another case, files disappeared. It got corrected, but looks like the detectives never received the new info. Shoddy, John, what can I tell you?" He sighed then went on. "Three more years, buddy. Retirement never sounded so good. Anyway, I have the updated file here." The sound of paper rustled before he spoke again, general noise of chatter and phones ringing in the background telling me he must have been at his desk. "Looks like poison, all right. Kid was murdered with something called kalmia latifolia. Stupid Latin. So, mountain laurel, found all over the north east.

Botanical, highly poisonous. Just traces in his test, but enough they said to kill him. Says here it screws up the heartbeat, brings on erratic contractions that end in death." More paper rustled and Bobby made a soft, angry sound. "Whatever, you know I don't understand the science stuff very well. Short of it, this plant shuts off the gate protecting the two sides of the heart from interfering with each other. And though it's a common plant, there's very little chance the kid could have accidentally ingested it or come into contact with it, being from the city and all. Unless he was dosed, and that's murder, buddy."

There was a bit more, a sign off, promises to get together at some point for beers when Dad was in Boston and then the inevitable hang up as the computer voice of the answering service asked me if I wanted to delete the message. I listened to it again, making sure I had all the details, before saving it for Dad and hanging up, staring at the paper in front of me.

So strange to look at the cute stationary Daisy got for me, a smiling pug face in the background with the horrible truth scrawled over her adorable features.

Manuel's murder confirmed. And now I needed to talk to Dr. Aberstock immediately.

CHAPTER THIRTY-TWO

INSTEAD OF THE LANDLINE, I reached for my cellphone, all the numbers I needed logged there. My finger hovered over Crew's for a long moment as I thought about sharing what Dad's friend gave us while my heart clenched against talking to him.

And how was I going to tell Emelia and Amos their son was murdered? Clearly that wasn't my job. But if the poison that killed Manuel showed up in Sadie, did that mean Emelia was the murderer after all? Or, if Sadie's death was from something different, was there a connection at all aside from the circumstantial?

That did nothing to mitigate the fact Manuel

Cortez was murdered. While his death happened elsewhere, I couldn't get past the fact his had to be connected. That led me right back to his mother.

I closed my eyes, forced myself to inhale, exhale, to still my pounding heart, to think about this and act responsibly rather than throwing myself into something that could make things worse. Look at me, being all grown up about it. Awesome.

Only then did I remember the text message from earlier, the one that interrupted my meeting with Dad and Crew. Turned out it wasn't a text after all, but an email. Pamela's name registered as I hastily checked what she'd sent, feeling my chest constrict further the more I read.

Sending this to Crew, too, but promised you the deets. Nice of her to remember, though I wondered if she told the sheriff she was sharing. *Prof's name was Gerald Phelpsy.* A photo of the man was embedded in the message. Handsome devil, youngish, charming, nice smile. *Disappeared end of term twenty years ago, no trace of him found. Here's the catch. Emelia Cortez was a suspect in his disappearance. According to sources, they fought all the time. She actually had two assault claims against her dropped by other female students in her department and it was common knowledge she and Phelpsy argued continually, often coming to blows. But he never called the cops and the administration swept it under the rug.* I'd witnessed her temper, the night of the séance, her huge reaction to Alice. I had no idea such outbursts were a regular occurrence, chalking it up to her emotional state. *The cops finally dropped the investigation into her because there was no proof against her. She had an alibi the night of his disappearance. Case went cold and was never solved.*

Did she kill her advisor and was never caught? But why? Too many questions still and not enough information to go on. I kept reading.

Now, about the son, and not the lovely-dovey relationship she led us to believe with her grieving mother act. Wait, act? It seemed real to me. I read on, coldness seeping into the pit of my already tight stomach. *The people I talked to said she controlled that kid from day one, from what he wore to what he ate to the training he took. And, from all accounts, it turned him into a spoiled, hateful brat no one wanted to work with.* Yikes. Amazing how the truth came out when rocks got flipped over. *Her family's money kept things quiet.* Emelia's family was wealthy? Not so shocking, really, from the way she carried herself, her demeanor, how she dressed. *I tracked down one of their old housekeepers and she was more than happy to talk after the fact. I guess Manuel and Emelia fought all the time, to the*

281

point the woman finally quit the night the kid threw one of his piano benches at his mother. Gulp. Not the impression Emelia gave me. Didn't sound like the kind of wonderful young man she'd made him out to be. *But here's the kicker. The night before his last concert he publically told his mother he was quitting, done playing and that he hated her, that she ruined his life. One of my reporter friends in Boston said she witnessed the blowup at the stage door of the theater, that they were screaming at each other on the street in Spanish. She told her son he'd be quitting over his dead body. Not hers. His.* That was a threat, all right, and didn't look good for Emelia. *Someone called the cops but she didn't know if anything came of it. The next night, the kid died. She took that info to the police but nothing came of it.*

I stared at that last line, frowning. Did the detectives not talk to her about their fight? Or did they just assume it was a mother/son spat? Dad's friend said it was a shoddy investigation. Maybe they looked the other way because her family had money? Whatever the truth, the deck was quickly stacking against Emelia Cortez. Whether she killed her son— and her advisor—in a fit of temper or in a calculated act of control, there was a lot hidden beneath her surface I'd clearly missed.

I sent off a quick thank you to Pamela before

pondering my next step. The search engine on my phone blinked, waiting for my input. I quickly sought out info on the poison, reading about the common plant and its effects on the body. According to the source I read, the plant had a bitter taste, especially when it was used by bees to make honey.

Wait. Honey? My mind flashed to Sadie, to the honey jar. To her excessive addition of sweetener to a single cup of tea. And to the jar on the tray in Amos's hands, Emelia's favorite brand she took with her everywhere.

I needed to get my hands on that honey.

Instead of running off as I usually did, I clenched my will power around the burbling need to dash and demand answers and instead did a search for Emelia. Came up with her listing at Harvard, but that was about it. No mention of the missing advisor, the history of her temper. Just a few smiling images of her and Amos at charity events, the occasional mention of the Diego family she was born to. Wealthy, my, yes. Her parents had a chain of dollar stores across the Northeast. Eyes burning from trying to navigate my smartphone, I realized I needed my laptop to do a more thorough search.

Okay. So honey as a possible delivery system.

Tied Sadie's death right to Emelia. Motive? Blackmail was one of the old woman's favorite methods of making money, right? Had Sadie uncovered something about Emelia that she was using against her? Was her son's death connected to the disappearance of her advisor?

Thinking back, was there any way someone could have slipped Sadie the plant? Yes, there was the honey, okay. Sadie was the only one to drink the tea, so it could have been in that if I wasn't going to jump to conclusions. Denver assured us it was a mix of store bought brands she passed off as fancy shmancy. Still, it would have been pretty easy to contaminate it in the darkness. I was sure Dr. Aberstock was having it tested anyway, so until I knew for sure, where else could the poison be sourced?

Question two, who sat next to her? From the report Bobby gave, the plant acted pretty quickly, so she had to have been dosed during the séance. Aundrea was on her right side, Pamela next to Aundrea. Unless the two lied, conspired over the deed and Pamela had her partner poison the woman, there was a good chance they were off the hook.

What about her left? I tried to picture the table and nodded to myself. Amos sat next to me, Emelia next to him and then Sadie.

I had yet to consider Amos in all this. How had he tolerated his wife's temper, his son's apparent abuse and horrible attitude? Poor man. What a tragic way to live his life. Though, as a lawyer, it was possible he might have been the reason the cops dropped the investigation against Emelia when her advisor disappeared, alibi or not. It was also possible he could have somehow influenced the investigation into his son's death to protect his wife. He did seem protective of her, but did that make him complicit or just a bystander trying to save what was left of his family?

My mind's eye dropped to the teapot next to Sadie as if I was there again and I watched in slow motion as the old woman stuck her spoon in a jar of honey again and again, excessive for that single cup of tea.

Memory flashed to the red label, that instant of recognition carrying me to Amos and his tray again. The same one, I was positive of it. The one Emelia was never without, according to her husband.

Grunt. I hated to suspect the woman, but honestly, it was really hard at this point not to. Fighting with her advisor the way she did, her history of a temper. And threatening her son's life, while all fed by excessive emotion, couldn't be discounted. If Emelia was as controlling as she sounded, the rage she showed might have been an act she used to hide a sociopathic nature. Coming here, making such a big show of trying to find out who killed her son might have been a part of the ruse to deflect suspicion. Not to mention getting her close enough to kill the woman who uncovered her secret. If she wanted to kill Sadie, using tainted honey was a great way to do it. Gift her the jar and make sure it was just available for her. Did she know the old woman wasn't going to share her tea with us? Did she care if others died, too? A sociopath wouldn't. That led me down the road to why Emelia would do such a thing and all I could think of was somehow Sadie knew Emelia killed Manuel.

Emelia's overwhelming grief. It must have been all an elaborate show. A grand performance to make sure she wasn't caught, but overdone to the point she left herself open to someone who figured out the truth. That led to the further question—was his rebellion enough to make her kill her own son?

One thing was certain as the cogs turned over and truths clicked into place. Things weren't looking good, were they? Again I reached for the phone, looked at Crew's number. He had to test the honey. Silly, of course he was already. He wasn't stupid. All the while anger grew inside me, frustration. There had to be a logical explanation. I couldn't be that bad of a judge of character, not after everything I'd been through.

Before I could stop myself, I was halfway across the foyer, heading for the stairs, determined to confront Emelia about the poisonings. Sure, it was dumb. More than dumb. If the woman was a rage-filled psychopath who murdered people for catching her in the act, I'd be making myself a target. Didn't stop me, though it should have.

Fate, as it would happen, had other ideas to keep me from doing something stupid. The front door opened, the hunched form of Oliver slipping inside, the sight of his scrunched and sad face making me pause as he held the photo I'd given him out to me in one shaking hand.

"Is it true?" He wept silently, voice hitching while he wiped the tears from his cheeks with the sleeve of his coat. "Is he my family?"

I have no idea where Alice came from, so intent on Oliver in that moment I missed her arrival. But she was there at his elbow, helping me guide him into the sitting room, placing him on the couch between us while I fetched the box of tissues and handed it to him.

Did it make me a horrible person I wished I could just get up and leave him to Alice while I went to confront Emelia? Yes. Yes, it did.

"As far as I know," I said, touching the edge of the paper with his image smiling back, "Denver is your grandson. You had no idea?"

Oliver shook his head, wisps of white hair shimmering like fluff around his face. "She told me the child was Patterson's," he said, though all the anger was gone from his voice, regret replacing it. He blinked at me, tears drying up but old hurt still there. "Why would she lie?"

"Maybe she didn't know how to tell you," I said, hating that I had to clean up the horrible woman's mess like this but doing my best to salvage as much of his dignity as I could. "She'd already told everyone the child was someone else's in an effort to blackmail his family." Yeah, great job with not making things worse, Fee. "Maybe she honestly didn't know." And stick the other foot in it, excellent.

Alice's eyes widened before she took over and I

floundered to a pathetic stop.

"We'll get a DNA test done," she said. "I know Denver will agree to it." Right, his thing for her. Likely he'd not turn her down for anything.

"My son or daughter." He cleared his throat. "Do you know where they are?"

"Maybe you should just talk to Denver." Weak, but better than blurting I was pretty sure his child was already passed on.

"I'd like to meet him." He snuffled, blew into a tissue with a loud honk. "I just don't know if I can face him alone."

"We'll take you." That's how Alice volunteered me to go to Sadie's without getting a chance to confront Emelia. I wanted to protest, but Oliver's reaction softened my heart and resigned me to helping him. After all, the living should come first.

Oliver hurried ahead of us as we exited the house, Mom rushing in past me in a flurry with bags in her hands, Petunia huffing at her side but Dad nowhere in sight. I slipped out with a brief shout to Mom I wouldn't be long, hoping I wasn't wrong at seven at night, my pug disappearing with her into the kitchen. I closed the door firmly behind me, knowing I was in a narrow window before Mom would want to go home.

I grasped Alice's arm on the walk, whispering to her, needing to tell someone what I'd uncovered. Screw Crew's suspicions. Alice didn't kill Sadie. Emelia did, I was positive of it. I'd only just finished unfolding the report from the detective as well as Pamela's email and my own suspicions when Alice grimaced pushing her glasses back, a faintly sick look on her face.

"I hate to add to your evidence against her," she said, "but you need to look further into Emelia's past." I waited for her to go on, though I wanted to turn around and run back toward the B&B, to confront the woman while Alice finished. "That advisor of hers who vanished? He wasn't a philosophy professor. She might be in that field now, but her original path of study was botany."

CHAPTER THIRTY-THREE

I STUMBLED IN SHOCK while Alice forged on, linking her arm with mine to help steady me, keeping her voice down when Oliver trundled on along ahead of us.

"You know by now I used to work for Sadie." She wrinkled her brow at me, nose scrunching as she admitted what looked like a failure if I was reading her expression right. "Yes, I thought so." My own face must have given her the confirmation she needed. "I know the sheriff thinks I'm a suspect because of my past with her and I'll admit there were times when I was living my jail sentence I wished she would die." Sounded like Pamela's admission, though without a hint of emotion behind Alice's words.

"When I was done, I made it my mission to track Sadie—I knew her as Marigold Hopp—and expose her as the fraud she was." Again, sounded like Pamela. From the blog Alice ran, she had a lot more success trailing behind the old woman and uncovering her activities.

"You didn't turn her in when you tracked her down." I didn't mean to sound accusatory at all. In fact, I knew in my heart Alice didn't do it—if my heart could be trusted.

She didn't take it that way, either, thankfully. "I was the one with the record," she said. "If I went to the police they'd be looking into why I was there in the first place. And the woman I now know was Sadie Hatch all along wasn't above turning me in if it meant she could move on and keep me off her trail."

How lovely of her. "How did you get mixed up with her in the first place?"

"It's a long story," Alice said before pausing to shake her head. "I've followed her from place to place, Fee. Investigated all of her clients."

"Did you ever find enough to go to the police?"

She flinched at my question. "Honestly, that was never my real intention." She swallowed like she knew that made her sound guilty. "I figured the cops would catch up with her eventually. That she'd rip off the wrong person at last. No, I've been looking for the means to warn her clients directly. That's what the blog was—and is—all about."

"Did you warn Emelia and Amos?" I waited for her answer with my whole body listening for wavering from the truth.

"I sent them a note," she said. "Anonymously. After I'd researched them and knew they were desperate for answers Sadie couldn't give them."

More evidence against Emelia. "You said Emelia was a botany specialist?" Who better to know the ins and outs of dangerous plants?

She nodded then. "It's not common knowledge, but she switched her discipline before her son was born. Though no one I asked could tell me why I suspect it had to do with losing her advisor."

Especially if she was the cause of the man's disappearance. Somehow tied to the death of Manuel and, I now believed, Sadie?

"Fee, I'm sorry I didn't tell you everything before." Alice's sorrow felt genuine. She squeezed my arm where she clutched it like that pressure would make me believe her. "I'm honestly just embarrassed. I was recruited young by Sadie, believed everything she told me. I wanted to help people, thought I was. Because…" she stopped then, not just her voice but her steps, pulling me to a halt next to her, just a few strides from the walk to Sadie's front door. "Fee, you're going to think I'm nuts, but." Her lips twisted into a small, crooked smile, eyes wary. "Sadie recruited me because I had a talent she didn't."

I waited for her to tell me what she meant, eyebrows raised while odd images of her juggling and folding herself into odd shapes flashed in my head for some reason.

Alice swallowed, looked down. "I have a gift," she said. "A paranormal gift. And Sadie used it to manipulate me and her clients."

My initial reaction was, of course, solid skepticism, though a thin tremor of holy crap ran through me. There was no time to ask her to elaborate, though, because Oliver was heading up the walk and Alice moving to join him. I rushed after her, feeling a shiver up my spine I immediately squashed. Poor thing was clearly deluded. Likely another side effect of working for Sadie. Though it did explain in part her obsession with the woman and her need to help Sadie's clients. If she thought she really was psychic or some such nonsense, she might feel compelled or guilty that Sadie took advantage of those Alice thought she herself could help.

Wow, and I thought I was screwed up.

I joined Alice and Oliver as he knocked, hand shaking but face eager. It was pretty clear he really didn't need me here and I almost retreated. I needed to talk to Crew after all, tell him about Emelia and let him question her. The door opened, Denver on the other side, and we were all being ushered into the front hall before I could leave.

Oh well, another few minutes wouldn't hurt. It was lovely to witness the moment of awareness on Oliver's face, how Denver looked at all of us with a bit of shock while the old man clasped him by the hand.

"I think," Oliver said in a voice that sounded happy for the first time since I'd met him, "I might be your grandfather."

Denver gaped, face pale before he pulled himself together. "Come in," he said, "join us for tea." It seemed like he didn't know what else to say.

Oliver followed him when Denver led him into the dining room while my mind whispered, "Us?" A questioning answered the moment we walked through the door and came to a halt to find Emelia Cortez lowering a spoon full of honey from a small jar with a red label into a cup of tea.

I moved immediately, without thinking, confiscating the honey, noting the teacup Emelia had been about to stir wasn't in front of her seat, but another. Holy Hannah, was she in the middle of poisoning Denver and we just saved his life?

The expression on my face must have spoken volumes because Emelia looked down at the cup and back to me with her own horrified expression. "What? What's happened?"

"I'll take that." I grasped the spoon, the honey now dissolved in the cup, shooing it to one side, too, protecting all of the items with my body. I fumbled for my phone, needing to call Crew, to get him here now, while Emelia looked at me with growing concern. When she reached out for me I froze, heart pounding. Was that the fury she'd unleashed on others deep in her eyes? Had I caught her red handed and she knew I knew?

"You killed Sadie," I said, shoving the honey jar in her face before she could blow her top, "with this honey." No proof of that, though, grasping at straws of accusation filled with hot air. I forgot to call Dr.

Aberstock. For all I knew, Sadie was poisoned by a bad batch of tea she made herself. I had zero anything behind that lie except conviction I was right. "And you used it to kill your own son. You were about to kill Denver with it. I just don't know why yet, whether you're a nutcase or did it in the heat of temper you can't control. But I'll find out. I promise you that." Never mind it was Crew's job to uncover the reasons why and all these clues. Forget it. This crap was personal now.

Rather than exploding as I expected, Emelia gasped like I'd slapped her. "My son?" There was the fake grief all over again. Man, she was a fantastic actress, I'd give her that. Except doubt then wormed its way into my heart while she lunged for me, grasping my upper arms and shaking me hard enough I dropped my phone. The rubber case bounced on the floor, skittering away out of reach. "What did you find out about Manuel?"

"Fee." Alice sounded like she was choking. "Stop."

But I couldn't, not now. I had to make her confess because now that she had warning, Emelia would be able to come up with an Oscar worthy performance by the time Crew got here. "Mountain laurel, Emelia," I said. Her eyes flew wide. "Found in your son's body. And in Sadie." That lie stung more than it should have, but whatever, I was on a roll. I jerked free of her and shook the honey at her. "And I bet when I have this tested—"yup, because I was the cops and all—"I'll find this honey is the murder weapon." Except Crew probably bagged the honey and the tea from the other night and this was a totally different jar. Whatever, not going to stop me. Exhale, gotcha, where's the handcuffs. "Tell me, did you also use it to make your advisor disappear?"

I fully anticipated her to hit me, to show that temper I knew now she used on others in her life. When Emelia broke down into sobs, sinking into a chair, I had a long instant of stunned surprise. Not buying it. Okay, so I was, guilt now awash inside me, clutching the honey jar and unsure what to do next. I caught a glimpse of my phone, saw it light up as Crew called. Remembered I wasn't actually a police officer and made a move to grab it. But Emelia caught my wrist and held me in place while Alice retrieved my phone and held it quietly in her hand, expression still and unreadable.

"I swear," the woman said. "I swear to you, I did not kill my son. Or that lying fraud. And there is no way I was going to kill Denver." She looked up, caught her breath, turned to meet his eyes. He stared in shock at her a moment before shaking his head at me. "As for my advisor, that was a long time ago. What does his disappearance have to do with this?"

"We were just going to have tea," Denver said. "I had some of the information my grandmother dug up about Manuel's death and I offered to share it."

Likely story. "Where's your husband? Back at Petunia's? Covering your tracks?" He could have been in on it but I doubted it now, felt sorry for the dupe she'd made of Amos. "Letting you slip out and come here to kill Denver?" Now I was starting to sound like a crackpot.

Have honey, will murder.

Emelia frowned a little. Where was her temper, then? Surely being confronted like this had to be a trigger, and yet she showed nothing close to flying into a fury. "I told Amos I was going for a walk. I just couldn't sit there any longer. And then Denver called, so I came here." Again she looked to him and again he confirmed her story with a nod. Likely story that actually sounded kind of likely.

Damn it.

"You're telling me it's just a coincidence your son

and Sadie were both killed by a botanical that you clearly know about because of your study history." There, take that, lie or not. "After your botany advisor mysteriously vanished without a trace, leading you to change your studies to hide your past?"

She swallowed hard, dabbing at her tears, face stiffening. "I was training to be a botanist," she said. "I know full well what kalmia latifolia is. But I assure you, I haven't had anything to do with botany for twenty years. Nor would I have any reason to kill my—" She froze, lights coming on behind her dark eyes.

In that moment, two things happened. First, her temper finally awoke, showing on her face as her cheeks flushed, gaze narrowing into a line of rage. And I had an epiphany, tied to her statement not so long ago when she told me Sadie knew Manuel something and didn't finish. Now I understood the old woman uncovered a secret Emelia only now connected to her son's death. In doing so she visibly awoke to who killed Manuel.

For the life of me, witnessing that truth dawn on her behind her fury, I couldn't bring myself to believe she was the murderer any longer. But neither did I have any idea who she suspected.

"Emelia," Alice said, voice soft, low. Almost threatening. I stiffened as she set my phone on the table, her entire body tense. When she met my eyes I almost squeaked in protest at the coldness there. While memory woke one last time and smacked me in the face.

That night. Of the séance. The cream and honey and skull holder for the napkins. Alice was the one who gave them to Sadie, moved faster than anyone else. I'd assumed it was out of a predisposition to be helpful. But what if it was to ensure the old woman took the poisoned honey? What if Emelia and Alice had met before, conspired together, the ex-con fraud and the murdering professor?

Alice's guilt had been there in front of me all along. Which meant I was only partially right. Alice killed them both, probably with Emelia's help. And they were going to kill us, too, to cover it up.

Emelia turned toward her partner in crime, terror on her face. Just as the lights went out.

CHAPTER THIRTY-FOUR

I COULDN'T BELIEVE IT. I'd been such an idiot. I dove for where I'd last seen Alice, the darkness swallowing everything. I crashed into someone, heard her grunt in protest, knew it was her, carried her to the ground.

"Fee, stop!" She struggled. "Get off me!"

No way was I letting her up. "Why? Why did you kill them, Alice?"

I can only imagine how ridiculous I looked, crouching over the young woman, her glasses askew from my tackle, when the lights came back on. Except, of course, no one was laughing because the figure in the doorway holding the gun on us kind of killed the humor of the moment.

"She didn't," Amos said, voice quiet and tired. "I did."

Wait, what? Alice pushed me off slowly and we both rose, though the gun followed our movements, Emelia rising to stand between us. I was now two people from my phone and in a whole lot of trouble.

Amos waved his weapon at Oliver and Denver, the pair sidling into the room further, covered firmly by the unwavering gun. He might have looked hurt and sorrowful, but there was nothing soft about the way Amos held us under threat.

"I didn't want this to happen." He was talking to his wife, not us. "But now that you know, you have to die, too."

"Why?" Emelia sounded like she already knew, her body shivering, hands falling to her sides. "Why my beautiful boy?"

My. Boy. I had my answer before Amos even spoke, kicking myself for not putting the pieces together.

"Your boy," he said and answered everything. As I remembered back to every conversation, every mention of Manuel. Always the use of his first name, without personal connection from Amos, the singular possessive from Emelia. The one time he called Manuel her son I should have realized the truth about the advisor and her switch in disciplines twenty years ago. Right around the time she got pregnant.

Not Amos's.

Idiot, Fleming. Some detective.

Emelia cried, but softly, shaking her head, while Alice sighed, meeting my eyes a moment with that same dull expression I mistook for guilt. Not coldness hiding murder, but regret for keeping more information from me.

"Manuel wasn't your husband's son, was he, Emelia?" She looked up to Amos who finally reacted physically, flinching. "He was your botany advisor's."

Had Alice known this, then, despite what she'd claimed? How much more had she kept from me?

"I could have forgiven your betrayal," he said to his wife. "I did, in fact, at the time of your adultery. And I even could have loved that boy as my own if I'd known the truth when you told me you were pregnant. Instead, you chose to let me believe the child you carried was mine. I had to find out during a blood test, Emelia." Fury rose in his voice. "A routine blood test six months after Manuel was born. I found out in my doctor's office the boy I thought was my child couldn't possibly be mine."

She vibrated like he'd struck her. "Amos." It was all she seemed able to muster.

"I hated him from that instant, Emelia. And you, did you know? Did you sense it? So wrapped up in that little disaster you created, that son who you doted on and ruined until he hated you as much as I did." Amos laughed, bitter, angry. "So I killed him," he said, casual, as if it had no consequence to his life. "I took away that child you fawned over and spoiled until he was useless, the boy that wasn't my blood." The gun shook with his emotion and fear shivered down my spine he could pull the trigger at any second. "He found out, Emelia, about your infidelity and his parentage. He knew. He was going to go looking for his real father." Amos stilled, shook his head. "The selfish, ungrateful little bastard would have ruined me, that pampered prince you made into a waste of breath." No love lost, was there? "He was blackmailing me, holding my whole life in his hands. My reputation." It seemed excessive, murdering the kid over Emelia's mistake. Was there more to this story yet? Emelia moaned softly, a protest that formed no words. "A heart attack. Simple and easy. No one would think to check for that compound, the simple plant I found in one of your old botany books, tucked in the attic, forgotten." His teeth flashed, a faint grin, humorless. "The detectives were friends of mine. Easy enough to distract them, to swap files." So not an accident after all, nor bad police work. Deliberate. "It should have been over, Emelia. I was willing to put it behind me. To continue my long game. My bench call is coming and I was going to wait just a bit longer. For the sympathy to work its magic and get me my robes. And then, I could finally kill you, too."

She froze then, still and cold. All grief left her in a flash of utter hate. "You bastard!"

He shrugged. "You use that word against me? Hypocrite." All his anger had apparently run out of him, leaving him empty, blank. "You made your bed. Die in it." The gun dipped slightly, his decision to fire so clear I blurted out a question to stop the inevitable.

"Sadie," I said. Amos's attention snapped to me, like he forgot I was there, any of us aside from his wife. "She was blackmailing you, too, about the death of Manuel." Amos nodded. "How did she find out?" I needed to keep him talking while I figured out what to do. Trouble was, there was nothing *to* do, except let my mind race and my heart too while Amos scowled.

"I don't know," he said. "But she did."

"I think that's my fault." Alice sighed. "In my investigation to protect you both, I uncovered some things that made me wonder if there was more to the story. Namely, your advisor's disappearance, Emelia, and the mysterious death of Manuel the police wouldn't call a homicide. I confronted her about what she knew, thinking she was involved somehow, or had a history with you. Sadie obviously put the pieces together I missed." Alice sighed softly. "She always was far too clever than was good for her. Educated guesses, without proof. But she came to you, didn't she, Amos? Told you she knew you killed Manuel and you panicked."

"She knew more than that." What was that supposed to mean? Hard to think, to wind through the clues and the confessions under such duress. Amos's jaw twitched, cords in his neck standing out a moment. My phone lit up again, bouncing softly on the table. When his gaze fell to it, his face settled back into calm. "I knew she had to die, too." His eyes met his wife's. "You were so surprised when I agreed to come to this miserable little town. So grateful." He choked on his own words. "You didn't know I came to pay her off in person."

"Instead, you killed her." I needed to get to my phone.

He grunted at me. "I had to protect myself."

"By setting up your wife," I said. "Making it look like she did it in case anyone figured out what really happened."

"You could have just stayed out of this." Alice glanced at me, though she was talking to Amos. "You could have let us believe Emelia did it."

But Amos shook his head. "The honey," he said, nodding to me. "You noticed it, brought it up. I was sure you knew." Irritation flashed over his face. "Clearly, I overestimated you." Thanks a lot. "I had no choice."

Betrayed by a jar of sweetener. And my bad luck wasn't a thing?

Emelia wasn't done. "What happened to Gerry, Amos?" She was shaking all over again. "That's the real reason you killed my baby, isn't it? To hide an older crime."

The last piece, of course. My mind made that final connection, the real trigger for Manuel's murder, as Amos shifted focus back to his wife.

"I couldn't very well let the man you cheated with live to tell about it," he said. "His disappearance was easy enough. Dark parking lot, late night ambush. They'll never find his body, Emelia." She didn't move, didn't breathe, while I struggled for my own gasp of air. "Without a body or any kind of proof of wrongdoing I knew you'd be fine. Made sure of it from my place in the prosecutor's office. Though part of me wanted you to go down for that, but I couldn't risk anyone looking at me. So I covered it up." He swallowed, free hand running over his face, making a rasping sound across the side of his beard. "The boy would have fallen into a rabbit hole I preferred to leave filled in. Asked questions that could have stirred up a renewed investigation. I couldn't have that." He seemed to struggle internally a moment. "I've lived with your lover's death for a long time. I wasn't sure I *could* live with it, but I did it. I told myself it was for my career, my future, our future. When you told me you were pregnant, that we were having a child, I forgave everything." Were those tears in his eyes? I couldn't bring myself to muster empathy for him while he held a gun on us, but still. "You betrayed me over and over again, Emelia. Ruined everything. I forced myself to endure, to live with it if only to ensure I didn't fall for your indiscretion."

"You just wanted my family's money." Emelia's bitterness flared, all of her grief gone to the temper that had gotten her into this mess in the first place.

Amos didn't argue. "I'll have all of it once you're dead. I'll finally be able to move on, the judge, the widow, the grieving father." That sounded like relief in his voice. Did he really think he'd get away with this? Considering the fact he'd avoided two murder charges, maybe he had reason to believe that. Small comfort to know Crew and Dad would never let it go because I'd be dead.

"What are you going to do?" I glanced at Alice, saw her hand twitch. Realized my phone was gone from the table. Who was the last person I dialed? Would they answer? Get the message? Please, let it not be someone silly, like the pizza place. Let it be Crew.

Who had I called?

"I'm going to clean up this mess once and for all." He backed away a step, hand reaching for the pocket door. "See, you *did* kill your lover, Emelia, in a fit of temper you're so famous for. When your son found out, the son you fought with constantly, the one who publically announced he was abandoning his career and blamed you for it, he blackmailed you, with her." He pointed the gun at Alice. "The others happened to be in the wrong place at the wrong time. Collateral damage. And then, of course, you couldn't live with yourself. So you ended it." He pointed the weapon at each of us as he went around the table. "Such a tragedy when insanity and depression claims so many lives, but unavoidable, I suppose."

"No one will believe it was a murder/suicide and that you weren't involved," I said.

"I suppose I'll have to risk that," Amos said. "Now, shut up, all of you. But, feel free to lunge for the gun. It will make the scene much more realistic when they find your bodies and pin this on my lovely wife."

This was it, we were toast. I tried to think of what to do, how to stop it, when Amos's finger closed slowly on the trigger, pointed at Emelia. I'd been here before, on the cusp of death. But never before had it felt so final, like the actual end. No Petunia to save me, no last minute rescue. Just the gun and Amos's determination to make his wife pay.

She screamed, I flinched, thinking the gun had gone off. Only to gape instead when the ghost of Manuel Cortez appeared.

CHAPTER THIRTY-FIVE

MOS CRIED OUT, STARTLED, the image of the dead young man hanging static beside him, shadowy and indistinct and unexpected. I found myself hurtling forward as the killer suggested despite knowing it was a terrible idea, arms outstretched while Oliver did the same. Amos swung the gun around to threaten the old man. Pinpricks of irritation, irrational at a time like that, spiked my temper that he'd chosen the old man as his biggest threat, not the redhead who was going to kick his ass. Just as soon as she died of fright for doing something as stupid as throwing herself at a loaded gun.

Again. Nope, not the first time.

Slow motion grasped me in cold, muffled hands, making the world feel like it had been washed over with slowly freezing ice, slushy pull of time wound down to almost nothing making my chest ache.

Denver pushed his grandfather to the side, out of the way, just as Amos's finger closed on the trigger for real and a bullet raced from the barrel. I'd been in life-or-death often enough the feeling of reduced time was familiar. It was my imagination, that things unwound at the normal pace of seconds ticking over, but I was positive I could track the course of that projectile as it flew through the air, just missing Oliver and Denver, embedding in the far wall to a shower of sparks.

The ghostly apparition of Manuel vanished, Denver's system shut down by a bullet. He must have triggered it somehow to try to distract Amos. It worked, at least. To a point. I was close enough to him he could have shot me instead, but was forced to agonize over the last few inches as, rage finally washing over his face, Amos shouted incoherently and spun the gun sideways. Aiming directly at his screaming wife.

I stumbled at the last second, tripping over the edge of the carpet, feeling myself falling, too late. I would miss and Emelia would be dead. Crew would never forgive me for this. Funny how that was the only real thought that mattered in the last few seconds of the woman's life.

Until Alice shrieked and Manuel appeared again. Not the static shape from Denver's system but the more active one he'd conjured the night of the séance. The bullet must have missed some vital part of operations because the new apparition moved fluidly, with his own rage on his face, perfectly rendered image of a furious Manuel Cortez, as he dove over me and directly through Amos.

Enough time, enough hesitation to push me that extra two inches required, scrambling to stay upright. Exactly what I needed to give me the breathing room to hit the man in the chest with my shoulder and knock him backward into the hallway and out of his wife's sightline.

Leaving me in the front entry with the crazy man with the gun. Awesome. Except he stumbled back, too, my forward momentum so much I simply couldn't catch myself from falling, and the two of us tumbled to the hardwood floor, his hand impacting the spindles of the staircase on the way down.

Another wild bullet hit its target as his grasping

hand pulled the trigger before the gun flew from his grasp, sliding over the floor toward the dining room. I shoved away from him, pushing myself backward in an effort to escape. He tried to grab me, faster than me, face a mask of madness, hands scrabbling for my throat.

I'd been here before too, not so long ago. Refused to let it happen again. Felt the barest touch of his fingers while I pushed with both feet, hurtling myself back and away from him, sliding over the hardwood on my butt as his fingers snapped shut on empty air.

My skittering progress ended abruptly as I came up against something soft but unyielding. Amos froze, looking up, over my head, face paling out, fury fading to terror. And, as I tilted my head slowly, registering my back pressed against someone's legs, I realized why.

Emelia held the gun in her shaking hands, mouth opening and closing, tears pouring down her cheeks and I knew in that moment if no one stopped her she would commit murder of her own.

Fortunately, Alice stepped to her side, took the gun gently, ever so gently, whispering soothing words to the grief-stricken woman who let her take the weapon from her before she strode across the distance at a rapid pace and kicked her husband firmly in the side as hard as she could.

Things devolved from there, Emelia shrieking in a mix of English and Spanish as her temper made a full-out appearance at last, beating her husband in a flailing attack of fists and high heels. I quickly got to my feet, Denver diving for her, pulling her off while the sound of a siren raced closer. I glanced at Alice, still in shock an unable to sort myself out, who showed me then the cellphone in her hand, mine, with Crew's name on the screen. Just as the door burst in and he appeared, his own gun out, shouting for Alice to put the gun down.

My hero.

I sat with Alice at the bottom of the stairs while Crew gestured for Robert to lead Amos out. The tall lawyer didn't look up, face grim, hands cuffed behind his back. He'd been silent since Crew's arrival, though his I'm sure soon to be ex-wife's vocal outpouring more than made up for it.

If she used the word "bastard" one more time, the irony of it would be just too much and I'd be laughing until I cried.

Patti Larsen

"I feel terribly for them." Alice was clearly blaming herself.

"You didn't do anything wrong," I said.

"I could have gone to the police, or even to Emelia herself." Alice tried a little smile that shook in the corners. "I'm tired, Fee. Of chasing ghosts." She laughed then. "At least, the ones Sadie created."

"Does that mean no more blogging?" It did make sense. Her main target was dead.

"No," she said. "But with Sadie gone, maybe it's time I looked at finding somewhere to call home." She glanced sideways, caught sight of Denver looking her way. And blushed.

Ah. Message received loud and clear.

Crew approached us with a frown on his face, but he sounded kind enough when he spoke. "Are you all right?"

I had no idea if he was talking to me directly, or included Alice, but it didn't matter which.

"Fiona saved us," Alice said, squeezing my hand. "If she hadn't tackled Amos and gotten the gun away from him he would have killed all of us before you could get here."

She might have been trying to help, but I kind of wished she'd just shut up because she was only

318

making things worse. At "saved us" he flinched. At "tackled" his expression darkened. And at "before you could get here" he actually looked away, breathing deeply, vein in his forehead prominent, cheek twitching, jaw tight.

Looked like the yelling would commence any second now.

Instead, he turned back to me, face set. "You have some things you need to tell me." Not a question.

I filled him in then on what Dad's friend told me, about my suspicions about the honey. "I wasn't coming here to confront her," I said. "We were here with Oliver." I hated having to defend that action, done out of kindness. I'd taken the right path this time and it still ended with me on the other side of that familiar look on Crew's face.

He grunted. "So you just happened to be in the wrong place at the wrong time again, is that it?" He waved off my protest. "I get it, Fee. Keep going."

Between Alice and me we shared what happened next and though I knew he'd already had this story from Denver and Oliver—nice of him to leave me for last—he listened intently like it was the first time.

When I was done, Crew was silent a long

moment, staring into my eyes. Here it came, the huge blow up, the jaw jumping and the disdain and frustration for my meddling. Instead, he reached out and squeezed my hand.

"I'm glad you're okay." And just like that, Crew walked away, joining Jill who was speaking with Oliver.

Huh. Well, I was glad, too, so I hoped he meant it.

Denver took Crew's place, checking us both over, especially Alice—okay, pretty much just Alice—before sinking shakily to a crouch.

"Just happy you two were here. He would have killed us both, I'm sure of it." He shuddered, rubbing his hands over his arms. Alice smiled at him, a sweet, secret smile, cementing my original conclusion about these two. Maybe something good might come of this mess, then. Not to mention Oliver finding his grandson. They would make an adorable family, if it came to that.

"You were pretty fast on your feet yourself." Alice's smile pinked her cheeks. "That was quick thinking."

I nodded agreement. "Great distraction. I hope your system is going to be okay." The bullet didn't help, but it was clearly still working, at least in part.

"That was just the prototype," he said. "The new one isn't built yet." He shrugged. "Hopefully I can salvage some of it, but I'm pretty sure it's toast."

"It did the job," I said. "Good thing you were able to get it working again the second time." I shivered. "Those static holograms are awesome, but the moving ghosts? You're going to make a fortune."

Why did Alice look suddenly anxious? While Denver shook his head, his face falling, offering me the remote he had tucked in his pocket. He hesitated then, shrugged. "Listen, the first time? Yeah, that was me." Alice didn't move, still uncomfortable. "But the second..."

"Wait," I said. "That wasn't you?" Um, what?

His focus was all Alice. "But you knew that already."

No. Way. No. It couldn't have been a real... Forget it. I had enough things whirling around in my head, at the limit of what I could handle at this particular moment. If it was a real ghost, if the spirit of Manuel Cortez chose to save his mother from the man who killed his father, so be it. Except, of course, that was totally crazy and despite Alice's personal belief about her so-called gift, wasn't true, would never be true and only meant I was on the fast track to a straightjacket for considering it.

Didn't stop me from sending out a tiny little thank you to whatever power was out there saved my butt. Because it couldn't hurt, right?

CHAPTER THIRTY-SIX

I SLIPPED TWO SMALL chocolate bars and two bags of chips into a pair of treat buckets while the kids holding them beamed and yelled, "THANK YOU!" so loudly Petunia barked. They bounded back down the steps to the street, matching kitten costumes adorable as they skipped away, parents waving and trailing after them.

I waved back before closing the door, my pug gazing with lustful longing at the basket full of goodies waiting for more kids to arrive.

It turned out to be a beautiful evening, perfect for the trick-or-treaters. We were almost at the end of curfew, the sun just fully set though long gone behind the mountains. While I made sure I had more than enough candy and goodies for my costumed visitors, I'd gone a bit overboard and would no doubt be partaking of too much sugar and salt before bed myself. What was one more night of junk debauchery for the fat ass of Fanny Fleming?

I turned to shed my witchy shoes—yes, I wore the same outfit as three days ago for lack of originality—as Mom burst through the door and hugged me so hard I was breathless a moment.

"They loved the samples!" She beamed at me when she shoved me away by a firm grip on my upper arms, bouncing on her toes. Not like her to be dressed in street clothes on Halloween, one of her favorite holidays, though the skirt and jacket she wore felt far more formal than even she'd become accustomed to wearing these days.

"That's great, Mom," I said, waving a bit to Dad who followed her inside, bending to pet Petunia, doing my best to muster enthusiasm while totally and utterly confused. "Who were and samples of what?"

Mom flushed slowly before laughing and shrugging to the ding of the doorbell. I answered it, handing out more treats, this time to a trio of teen girls dressed like zombie cheerleaders. They chorused their gratitude before giggling over Petunia on their way out. I left the door ajar for a pair of my guests, returning from a wander around Reading, forcing treats on them with a grin. I spun as they went upstairs to find Mom and Dad whispering heatedly behind me.

"Okay," I said. "You already spilled part of the beans. Out with it. What's up?"

"Don't you dare tell a soul." Mom's elevated whisper could have been heard in the kitchen. "Pamela and Aundrea." She beamed again, this time at Dad then at me as he smiled indulgently. "They asked me to make their cake. For their wedding!" I suspected as much, though I still wondered about the reaction Pamela gave me when I'd asked her after her confession over her connection to Sadie. Was it really just yesterday? "And they loved what I made for them." She was practically dancing in place, hands clasping in front of her.

"The super secret project, I take it." She didn't need me to ruin her excitement by telling her I guessed. I grinned and Mom stopped suddenly, anxious.

"I just couldn't keep in in anymore." She tensed. "You won't say anything, will you, Fee?"

"Of course not." I hugged her, kissed her cheek.

"That's awesome, Mom. How fun. And I'd be shocked if they didn't love your cake."

Her excitement returned. "Oh, Fee, this is the beginning, I know it. I have to tell Daisy!"

She rushed toward the kitchen like she was on fire while Dad chuckled after her.

"I've never seen her so happy," he said. "This is good for her." Why then did he look sad all of a sudden? Was he thinking about Crew's offer, by any chance? Memory pinged, his reaction and I wondered then why he'd been so upset. I'd have to ask. In the meantime, had he mentioned it to Mom? She'd been happy he retired. Maybe that was his reason for being so angry? I couldn't see my mother being the source of so much temper, though. Dad always did what Dad wanted.

I didn't get to ask him because he was already following after her and, honestly, my real attention was elsewhere. I bit my lower lip and tried very hard not to feel hurt Mom ran off to share her secrets with someone else.

Specifically, with Daisy. She knew all about Mom's project and hadn't told me. I shook that off, mentally smacked myself. First of all, it was a secret and not theirs to tell. Second, Daisy had been helping

Mom because I didn't have time. I knew that already. Mom made a few cakes for her, did some light catering for a couple of her other events. And third, I was so into snooping around where I wasn't supposed to poke my nose I'd missed out on being in Mom's confidence.

Still. Hurt just a little. Sigh.

The clock in the foyer struck eight, curfew officially in place. I stepped out onto the porch for a peek down the street to make sure no one else was coming and paused, eyes locked on Peggy's next door.

I had my own secret. One that I needed to share with my parents, I guess. Since I'd already decided I was going to buy it, gone to the bank this morning to make arrangements to do it myself. Not that I didn't want to partner with Jared and Alicia, but some things needed to stay in the family. Confirmation came this afternoon, the very reasonable mortgage offer Jared made me approved.

I'd be signing the paperwork the first of the week. Which meant not only was Vivian going to be ridiculously upset that Mom scooped the wedding of the decade—Aundrea was a Patterson after all—but that I killed her plans for a hotel, if only for this year.

Whoops. My bad. Let's see what kind of takedown she'd try next because I was so ready for her it hurt.

I turned to go back inside, to talk to Mom and Dad and inform them their daughter had officially lost her mind, only to run into Daisy. She hugged me as if she'd been searching for me everywhere then let me go, breathless.

"You're buying it, aren't you?"

Wait, how did she…? I couldn't help the tug of irritation that jerked my brows together.

My best friend blanched and backed up a step, hand covering her open mouth. "I'm sorry. I didn't mean to spoil the surprise. Jared and Alicia told me you were thinking about it."

"Did you tell Mom and Dad?" That was harsher than I wanted.

Daisy immediately shook her head, horror in her eyes. "Fee, no! Never. I'm sorry." Again with the apology. The crust of nastiness that formed around my heart broke away and fell free as I hugged her this time.

"No, I'm sorry." I let her go, leaning against the post of the porch, staring into the darkness. "Thank you. It's been a rough few days." Had it. Crew hadn't yet talked to me, though I wasn't surprised by that. And maybe I was avoiding him and the inevitable continuing of his disappointment. Or maybe buying the annex would lighten our relationship a little? Surely I'd be far too busy now to poke my nose into his police work.

Daisy looked wistful. "And I wasn't here to help you yesterday." She'd been working at the Lodge for Jared and Alicia, their own Halloween soiree for guests, hardly cause to feel guilty for missing out on almost getting shot, too. "You're doing the right thing, you know."

If she said so. I cracked a smile. "I'm nervous and probably mental, but I'm doing it anyway."

She squealed a little, vibrating with the excitement I should have been feeling right then. "That's so amazing, Fee. It's going to be incredible, don't you think?" She turned toward Peggy's—mine, soon enough—and sighed. "You're going to need more staff." Wait, was she fishing? I jumped on the chance, all animosity long gone with the hope that scurried like a trapped animal inside me.

"Was that an offer?" I would not beg, but neither was I above asking. I shook my head almost immediately, knowing better than to do this to her.

She had her own thing now and I'd told myself not so long ago her happiness had to come first. "My turn to apologize. I know how much you love your new gig. You're doing a great job event planning."

"Actually." She hesitated. "I was going to ask you if you needed anyone. Not that I don't appreciate I've found something I'm good at!" Daisy laughed then. "Just, there's not many events to plan in a small place like this. And I love Petunia's so much, Fee. I've missed it, being here every day."

Relief flooded me and I finally found my excitement. "Really? You want to work here again?" That would be a huge load off my mind. Yes, she was a bit scatter brained but the guests loved her and I could rely on her no matter what. Why had I been mad at her again? Felt hurt my mom and she shared a secret?

Silly Fee. Daisy was family, too.

To prove it, she burst into tears and hugged me. "Fee," she hiccupped. "Petunia's, you, your parents? You're home."

Wow. She let me go abruptly, laughing away her brief stint of weeping, brushing at her tears while I absently blotted my own with the sleeve of my witch costume. Maybe I was alone when it came to having a partner in my life, but I was far from on my own.

I drifted back inside, closing the door, carrying the basket of treats to the kitchen, thinking about the annex and where to go from here. How the ladies would fit in, if they even would want to stay with the extra work involved. What would Mary and Betty say? Okay, what would Mary say while Betty stayed characteristically quiet? I'd have to visit them tomorrow and make sure they heard of the annex purchase from me.

Calling it that led me to a revelation. "We need a name for it," I said abruptly.

Daisy paused before we joined my parents, a little frown forming but not the unhappy kind, more serious and thoughtful. "Not Petunia's the Second?"

I laughed at that. "No, I have some ideas about how to make it more... I don't know. Different. So it needs its own name." I couldn't call it the annex forever.

Daisy brightened. "Might be a silly idea, but maybe we could look at those letters you found." She flushed a bit. "The love letters." Right, the ones Grandmother Iris kept in the box I'd uncovered in the garden. "It might be fun to read through them, to see if there's something in them that tells us about the annex. Inspiration?"

"I think Grandmother Iris would love that."

Daisy looked like she wanted to say something, as if she wasn't telling me everything. She was such an open book, it wasn't hard to spot she had a motive outside the one she'd mentioned.

"Okay, fine," she blurted as if I'd pressed her to reveal the truth though I didn't say a word. "I want to look at them for hints about the treasure." Now she was really blushing.

I laughed out loud. "You could have just said." I had enough mysteries of my own without worrying about some make believe hoard, doubloon or no doubloon. I handed her the basket of treats and retreated to my apartment, fishing the letters out of the drawer in my nightstand, pausing to stare down at the music box with the envelope stack in my hand.

Locking my gaze on the card with the name scrawled in Malcolm Murray's handwriting.

Yeah, I had more important mysteries to sort out. As soon as I got up the courage to find out who Siobhan Doyle was and why her connection to Dad made me feel so uncomfortable. To visit Oliver's shop, ask him what he knew now that he rather liked me for helping him connect with Denver. When I was ready to face such questions without feeling like I was betraying my dad.

Weird how it felt that way. I didn't have qualms snooping about other things, did I? Why then did getting answers, the opportunities presented to me making it rather simple comparatively, suddenly feel like I could barely breathe past the sight of Malcolm's firm handwriting on the card?

I reached for it. Ran my fingertips over the name, touched the edges with shaking fingers. Before sliding the white rectangle inside the secret compartment of my grandmother's music box. I closed it firmly with a faint sigh. Nodded to myself like such a gesture helped.

Headed upstairs to the sound of laughter, choosing to love my family and my life, drama be damned.

This mystery could wait one more night.

The Reading Reader Gazette

VOLUME 1   ISSUE 1   NOVEMBER 2ND, 2018   WWW.RRGAZETTE.COM

News Briefs

1. **Town Hall Christmas Party:** In conjunction with Reading Town Council, the Reading Christmas Party is in full planning swing and needs volunteers! Please contact Joanne at the front desk for information.

2. **Parking Violations:** Your town council would like to remind you that parking restrictions for the fall and winter season begin on November 1st and will continue until April 1st. Any Reading resident whose vehicle is found parked outside their driveway or on town property, taking up valuable parking space for visitors, will be towed at their expense. Let's keep Reading's streets open for our tourists!

3. **History of Reading Reading:** Join local historian Oliver Watters at the Reading Town Library on Friday evening from 7-9PM for a breakdown of his most recent work, *Reading the Scoundrel: A Pirate's Life at Sea.* Tea and lunch will be served after the event.

4. **Statue Vandalism:** The Sheriff's department in conjunction with Town Hall would like to encourage anyone who witnesses vandalism of our Captain Reading statue to please report in to local law enforcement.

While mildly amusing, the phallic addition to our venerable founder and frequent spray painted vulgarities are expensive to remove and aren't a reflection of our town's tourist strategy. Thank you!

Winner of this week's Fire Hall 50/50 draw: Betty Jones. Congratulations, Betty!

Please send any pending community notices to: pamela@rrgazette.com before 4PM.

Murder Haunts Reading

Boston lawyer Amos Cortez is being held for the murder of Harvard professor Dr. Gerald Phelpsy (42); star pianist prodigy Manuel Cortez (19) and local psychic Sadie Hatch (64) in a bizarre triangle of love, loss and betrayal.

Local soothsayer killed by murderer she tried to blackmail

By Pamela Shard

By all accounts driven to murder first for love, twice for money and finally for revenge, former assistant district attorney and Boston law partner Amos Cortez, 50, has been arrested in connection with the deaths of Harvard botany professor Dr. Gerald Phelpsy, his wife's son, pianist Manuel Cortez, and recent returned resident Sadie Hatch in a complex plot of death, adultery, blackmail and ambition spanning twenty years.

Boston police are cooperating fully with the Curtis County Sheriff's Department, though it is likely Mr. Cortez will return to Massachusetts to answer for his crimes in that state before any proceedings against him can be carried out in the state of Vermont.

"I have no problems with extraditing him to another jurisdiction to stand trial," Sheriff Crew Turner told the Gazette. "If, for some unforeseen reason, he isn't convicted of the two murders out of state, you can be sure the case against him for Ms. Hatch's murder will

be air tight. My team is hard at work to ensure all evidence against Mr. Cortez is prepped and ready. I'm positive no matter what happens in Boston, justice will be served."

The sheriff refused to comment on the continuing assistance he's received from the Fleming family, including rumors of the information handed to him from former Sheriff John Fleming, retired, as well as his daughter, Petunia's Bed and Breakfast owner, Fiona.

"The Flemings continue to be a valuable and supportive part of our community here in Reading," Mayor Olivia Walker said. "We're very grateful for their assistance."

When asked if the increase in crime could be connected to the growing tourist industry in Reading, however, Mayor Walker declined to respond.

With the outcome yet to unfold in the case of Sadie Hatch's untimely murder, it remains to be seen if such occurrences will increase.

Neither John Fleming nor Fiona Fleming were available for comment at the time of printing.

COMING SOON, THE NEXT in the Fiona
Fleming Cozy Mysteries series…

AUTHOR NOTES

THIS BOOK IS A partial nod to my past, to the paranormal that normally haunts the books I write. I started out in hard core sci-fi and heroic fantasy so many moons ago I can't recall the number. Back when I was a wee lassie who wanted to play Dungeons&Dragons every day and never, ever come back to the real world.

When I switched to young adult paranormal in my late thirties, I thought I'd never leave. Writing about witches and demons, vampires and werewolves, and all the fun of the supernatural world gave me the kind of thrill I wasn't expecting.

Exploring horror, post-apocalyptic, jaunting back to sci-fi and fantasy, I typically had some kind of paranormal element, even when I tried to stay true to genre (I'm looking at you, lonely romance novel with a ghost in it…).

But with Fiona, I found a voice less magical, but no less extraordinary. I adore her and her family, her life in Reading. And while it was fun to dip her toes into a story that shared a thread of the spooky, hers isn't the world of the Hayle coven or the Sick or the hunters, nor the Horizon, without cyborg gunslingers or a fantasy world more game than reality.

And yet... I hope you had fun and that, like Fee, Manuel's ghost made you wonder.

Happy sleuthing!

Best,
Patti

ABOUT THE AUTHOR

EVERYTHING YOU NEED TO know about me is in this one statement: I've wanted to be a writer since I was a little girl, and now I'm doing it. How cool is that, being able to follow your dream and make it reality? I've tried everything from university to college, graduating the second with a journalism diploma (I sucked at telling real stories), was in an all-girl improv troupe for five glorious years (if you've never tried it, I highly recommend making things up as you go along as often as possible). I've even been in a Celtic girl band (some of our stuff is on YouTube!) and was an independent film maker. My life has been one creative thing after another—all leading me here, to writing books for a living.

Now with multiple series in happy publication, I live on beautiful and magical Prince Edward Island (I know you've heard of Anne of Green Gables) with my very patient husband and six massive cats.

I love-love-love hearing from you! You can reach me (and I promise I'll message back) at patti@pattilarsen.com. And if you're eager for your next dose of Patti Larsen books (usually about one release a month) come join my mailing list! All the best up and coming, giveaways, contests and, of course, my observations on the world (aren't you just dying to know what I think about everything?) all in one place: http://smarturl.it/PattiLarsenEmail.

Last—but not least!—I hope you enjoyed what you read! Your happiness is my happiness. And I'd love to hear just what you thought. **A review** where you found this book would mean the world to me— **reviews feed writers** more than you will ever know. So, loved it (or not so much), **your honest review** would make my day. **Thank you!**

69686561R00190

Made in the USA
Middletown, DE
08 April 2018